STO

CLASSMATES BY REQUEST

by the same author
THE BEST WEDDING DRESS
A CROWN FOR GINA
THE GIRL FROM PUERTO RICO
JULIE BUILDS HER CASTLE
MRS. DARLING'S DAUGHTER
PHOEBE'S FIRST CAMPAIGN

CLASSMATES
BY REQUEST

hila COLMAN

william MORROW AND COMPANY
NEW york 1964

jC713cl

u. S. 1269031
for louis

CLASSMATES
BY REQUEST

CHAPTER 1

THE IMPOSING grandfather clock in the hall was striking six. Carla turned down the fire under the stew and ran upstairs to her room to change her clothes. Dressing for dinner was a ritual for her, part of the tradition she had been keeping ever since her mother's death. Her mother used to make an occasion of dinner, dressing in low-cut silks and chiffons, her hair piled high on her head, her quick, slim hands sparkling with rings. "I don't want to look like a scullery maid for my husband," she used to say laughingly. "I want to be as beautiful as I know how."

Carla had also inherited her mother's unashamed adoration of Carla's father. Jake Monroe was a man to adore, but not an easy man to love. There is a difference, Carla thought. When you love someone you want to feel close to him, be able to touch spontaneously, to be silly and careless if you feel like it. But there were few easy, thoughtless moments with Mr. Monroe. His sharp eyes saw everything, things Carla sometimes hoped he would miss, and he had no pa-

11

tience with sloppy, make-do short cuts. He had a reputation in town for being tough. Opposing lawyers worked doubly hard when they came up against Jake Monroe in a trial, but his clients, like Carla and her mother before her, worshiped him.

It was the toughness of his integrity that they admired; Mr. Monroe lived by his principles. "I submit to compromise," he was fond of saying, "but not if it's an excuse for abandoning the things I believe in."

Neither Carla nor her mother, nor Carla's younger brother Dan, had ever questioned Mr. Monroe's principles. They took for granted that he preferred representing a poor workingman, rather than a wealthy corporation, and accepted the fact that more often than not his fee might never be paid. The Monroe family never gave a thought to the world Mr. Monroe had chosen not to inhabit, the world of the rich and successful, with their country club and big ranch houses set in parklike grounds around the lake. "Let them have their luxury," Mr. Monroe said. "I like my old house, and I'm not worried about Negroes for neighbors. Do us good. Do us all good."

Carla wasn't sure she absolutely agreed with her father about the old Victorian house. It was a lot to take care of, with its ten rooms (some of which Carla finally convinced her father they should shut off), its ornate mantelpieces, floors that needed constant waxing, huge sideboards, and china closets containing her mother's collection of lusterware. Sometimes Carla longed for a new modern house where the dust had no place to accumulate and all the rooms were on one floor. But she knew she would soon get tired of a house that didn't have unexpected twists and turns, a wide gracious stairway, and a cherished window seat on the stair landing where she could curl up when she wanted to look out and think.

"Hey, Carla, something smells good." It was Dan banging the front door as he came in downstairs, his new deep man's voice still coming as a surprise. "Company for supper?"

"One of Dad's young men."

"A waif or a wafer?" This was a joke between them. Mr. Monroe was in the habit of bringing home stray people, more often than not someone in need of a good, home-cooked meal. However, since he was also active in various community enterprises of the energetic eastern Pennsylvania city in which they lived and he practiced law he was as likely as not to turn up with the president of the bank, a university professor, or a judge. Carla and Dan separated the starving strays from the well-fed guests by privately calling them waifs and wafers.

"I have a hunch this one's a little bit of both." Carla came out of her room, tying the cord of her bathrobe tightly around her, and leaned over the stairs to talk to Dan. "He's a law student at the university, and I think Dad's taking him into his office on part time. Dad said he was brilliant."

"Do I have to wear a tie for dinner?" It was a routine question. Dan was unimpressed by his father's friends. Carla marveled at the poise of her fourteen-year-old brother. He took everyone in his stride and was able to discuss nuclear physics with a bearded Ph.D. as easily as he talked about the Mets with his friends from school. I wish I could be like that, Carla often thought. Too often in the presence of her father's friends she was afraid to open her mouth, feeling left behind by their quick, informed minds. "You're just as smart as they are," Dan told her often. "I just put up a bluff with them. It's easy—a lot of the time they don't know so much themselves."

"They know more than I do," Carla would say. Although she had to admit that often someone else would say exactly what she had been thinking, but hadn't had the nerve to say out loud. Then she'd be sorry she hadn't spoken up. Knowing the answers, but not having the confidence to give them, or not being sure enough she was right, seemed to Carla just as stupid as not knowing them at all. What was the use of knowing something if she kept it to herself? Then the knowledge is wasted, like a book that's never been read, Carla thought. And Carla hated waste. She couldn't stand wasted food, wasted money, wasted energy, or wasted brains. Carla and her father had this belief in common: they both felt strongly about seeing people make use of their talents, which accounted for many of the waifs that Mr. Monroe became attached to. If a person had any special gifts, Mr. Monroe drove him passionately to use them. And Carla did the same, to everyone except herself. Her friend Twinkey was a girl with gifted hands, who could draw, paint, hang wallpaper or, with a twist, turn an old hat into a chic creation. Carla was always after her to work at her art, to be disciplined. But Twinkey was lazy. With her wide, innocent gray eyes, she'd look at Carla and say, "What about you? Why don't you do something?"

"Because I can't," Carla told her emphatically. "I have no talents."

"Your talent is that you're so well organized," Twinkey said.

Carla didn't *feel* well organized. Between running the house for her father and Dan and being a senior in high school, she always left many things undone. She had Hattie, who used to work for her mother, come in to clean and do the cooking a couple of afternoons a week, but Hattie was more of a good friend than a servant, and Carla didn't feel that she should tell a much older woman what to do. As a result there was

15

always a pile of ironing accumulating in the pantry, at least one china closet (which her mother used to keep shining) accusingly covered with dust, and mending, such as Dan's socks, to be done. Thank goodness her father refused to wear darned socks. He said it was a waste of good time mending them, and besides they were always lumpy anyway. But Carla couldn't get herself to throw out Dan's when they were perfectly good except for one little hole.

She could hear Dan now turning on the kitchen radio for the football scores, and she knew he'd be munching on a handful of cookies. She should tell him not to eat before dinner, but what was the use? He'd answer, as he always did, that he'd still take seconds on everything for dinner, and he'd be right. Parents threw out so many pat phrases automatically, as if saying them fulfilled some inner need of theirs, although both they and their children knew they were meaningless. Foolish, impossible things like "Don't get wet," "Take care," "Go to bed early," "Don't worry," and "Don't eat before meals." What was the difference if Dan ate a peanut-butter sandwich or all of his dinner? Peanut butter was nourishing too!

Carla brushed her shoulder-length blond hair conscientiously before putting on her printed cotton, her favorite dress, which tied with a flat bow in high, Empire fashion. She wanted to look as nice as possible.

Her father hadn't said anything, but by a few questions he had asked—What were they having for dinner? and Was she going to make a dessert?—Carla guessed that he wanted to make a good impression on the young man he was bringing home. Besides Gadge Conefry, a boy she was dating, had said he might drop around after dinner.

Gadge was a narrow, wiry boy, only a little taller than Carla, whose serious, intellectual face was saved by a pair of very bright, light, almost hazel eyes. His eyes lit up his whole face, and contrasted strongly with his dark sun-tanned skin and his closely cropped black hair that lay like a cap on his head. He always walked around with a couple of paperbacks sticking out of his pocket, one of them poetry, usually Keats or Shelley, and the other possibly Salinger or William Golding. But Gadge was not a snob, and had been known to stay up nights helping less well-endowed students prepare for an exam. Everyone respected Gadge, and most people liked him. He did not try to hide his intellectual interests, and could laugh at the wisecracks that were made about him with a sincere and unaffected enjoyment.

Carla wondered why she was not in love with Gadge. She loved being with him. She could talk to him, they could argue about everything and anything, she liked kissing him, and they could laugh at the same ridiculous things. But she wasn't *in* love with him. Even though she had never been in love, as she said to Twinkey, she still knew when she was *not* in love. Something was missing.

Carla had the salad made, the cream whipped for dessert, and was dressed and ready by the time her father and his guest came home. Although the September day had been hot, it was a cool evening, and Dan had lit a fire in the high-ceilinged, large living room. It was a somber room, with rather a musty air to its dark, Victorian furniture, its damask drapes and faded rugs. Every once in a while Carla had an urge to brighten it up with white paint and new curtains, but her father didn't want her to touch it. He never said why, but Carla knew it was because he connected the room with her mother, and he wanted the house kept exactly as her mother had furnished it with the antiques she had enjoyed picking up at auctions.

Carla was glad for this unexpected streak of sentiment in her father, it made him more human and lovable, and she often had to remind herself of it. He was wonderful at expressing ideas and talking about them, but he seemed totally inarticulate about his feelings. Sometimes Carla wondered if they were so deep and complex that he, himself, didn't quite understand them. Her mother had died when she was eight, and Dan only five, and while she had a clear memory of her

18

(with the help of photographs) she had been too young to be aware of the relationship between her mother and father. It was a source of great speculation for Carla, and the subject of many conversations between herself and Twinkey. Had her parents been very much in love? What had they been like together? Carla couldn't really picture her father in love with a woman, especially someone whom she remembered as being frivolous, gay, almost scatterbrained.

The quiet atmosphere in the house changed the minute Mr. Monroe walked in. He was full of motion and action, and he carried a constant air of excitement with him. "Hello, Carla, Dan. I want you to meet Adam Blake. Adam's going to work for me this year. He has a few courses to finish at the university, and he has to prepare for his bar exams in May. I don't know when he's going to have time to sleep, I have so much for him to do."

"I guess I won't be sleeping much this year," Adam said with a smile. "Sleeping's a waste of time anyway. I'll catch up on it when I'm an old man."

Adam spoke in a low, quiet voice. Carla thought he must be around twenty-three or twenty-four. In physical appearance he was the exact opposite of her father. Mr. Monroe was short for a man, not fat but stocky, with a strong, energetic body and face. His features were large and well shaped, but everything about him was a trifle exaggerated, his nose a shade too big, his eyes too deeply set, his chin outthrust. Adam was tall and slim, with a quiet manner, a wide sensitive mouth, serious gray eyes. But he, too, had a stubborn chin, and Carla sensed that this young man could be just as tough and uncompromising in a fight over principles as her father.

"Want a drink?" Mr. Monroe asked Adam.

"No thanks."

Mr. Monroe mixed himself a short highball as he did every night before dinner. "Supposed to relax me." He grinned at Adam. "Maybe it does, I might be worse without it."

"At least sit down while you're drinking it," Carla suggested, watching her father pace in front of the fire with the glass in his hand.

"I've got a lot on my mind. What did you think of that bunch?" he asked Adam abruptly.

"I think they mean business. I'm for them, and I think they're absolutely right."

"Of course they're right. We all know that, and it's high time they did something about it. But how far will they get? That's the point. Take a look at the school board, and you figure it."

At the words *school board,* Carla's eyes became alert. "What's going on? Can't you tell us?"

"Yes," Dan echoed, "tell us what you're talking about."

"George Randall and some of his friends dropped in to my office this afternoon. They're going to boycott the new school down the block here. They say it's segregated." George Randall was Hattie's nephew and an old friend of Mr. Monroe. One of the leaders of the Negro community, he taught at the school in the Negro neighborhood, and he and Mr. Monroe had worked together on various committees for civil rights.

"Of course it's segregated, it's the same as the old one," Dan said. "Are they just waking up to the fact?"

"No, of course not," Mr. Monroe said sharply. "I think they know it as well as you, young man. Perhaps they haven't been able to do anything about it before, ever think of that?"

"You don't have to jump on me." Dan's face flushed.

"Of course not. I'm sorry." Mr. Monroe tousled his son's hair affectionately. "But the school problem is not an easy one." He shook his head angrily. "The Negroes in town had high hopes that the new school would be different. Their idea is that it should be a combination junior and senior high school. The school you kids go to should be the elementary school. They say it's ridiculous to operate two separate twelve-grade schools. It means double on everything and more expense to the city."

"The plan makes sense, but why didn't they bring it up before? Why are they starting now?"

Carla looked from her father to Adam.

"It takes time to develop leaders," Adam answered her. "They seem to have them now. A lot of things are happening all over the world today that never happened before."

Mr. Monroe nodded. He'd be sore as anything if Adam disagreed with him, Carla thought irrelevantly. There was a mischievous gleam in Adam's eyes, as if he, too, were well aware of this fact.

"Let's eat," Dan said.

"Yes, dinner is ready." Carla stood up. She caught Adam's eye as she turned toward the kitchen, and had a sudden, intuitive feeling that he was thinking the same thing that she was: here they were in their cozy, firelit room, about to eat a good dinner, when just down a block or two there were families living in despair, people who might hate them, consider them their enemies. But Hattie wouldn't think that, Carla thought reassuringly. Surely Hattie must know that we love her and wish her well, that we don't care about the color of her skin. But it wouldn't be Hattie who would be boycotting the school!

After dinner Dan went off to see a friend. Adam insisted on coming into the kitchen to help Carla with the dishes. Carla wished she knew how to ask him all the questions about himself that she was sure Twinkey would want to know: Where did he live? Who was his family? When had he come to Thomasville? Did he have a girl?

But Adam said very little about himself other than that his family lived in California, and he had a little apartment of his own near the university. If he had a girl, he didn't mention her. Carla wondered about him. He was by far the most attractive young man her father had ever brought home. As a matter of fact, she realized, as she watched his tanned, fine hands dry their best dishes, he was the most attractive young man she had ever met.

Carla was sorry when Gadge arrived and suggested a walk, for there was nothing to do but go along. She would have much preferred to stay and listen to the conversation between Adam and her father. They would talk about ideas, about books, about world events. . . . Suddenly Carla was dismayed by her own momentary self-delusion. Gadge could talk as well as anyone, so that wasn't what made her reluctant to leave . . . the truth was she really wanted to get to know Adam Blake better!

CHAPTER 2

By SEVEN-THIRTY in the morning, Hattie Randall had accomplished a full day's work. She had washed and hung out three tubfuls of clothes; she had scrubbed her kitchen floor, ironed three crisp little dresses for her youngest grandnieces, and made a huge bowl of pancake batter for breakfast.

"The trouble with you is, you have too many vitamins. What do you accomplish with all this cleaning and scrubbing? Everything gets dirty again anyway." George Randall still had sleep in his eyes as he poured himself a cup of Aunt Hattie's strong black coffee. He was a slim, tired-looking man, at forty appearing to have seen about as much of the world as he cared to. The small lines around his eyes and mouth, however, were more those of amusement than of sadness.

"Don't give me that foolish talk." Aunt Hattie heaped a mound of pancakes on a plate and handed it to Mr. Randall. "You used up all my hot water taking a shower for half an hour. Why do you wash yourself so much, you only get dirty again?"

The two of them grinned at each other with affection. Aunt Hattie had brought up George Randall, and was a mother to him as well as a grandmother to his four daughters. She had lived with him and his family ever since he'd been married, working hard, bossing everyone, and loved by all.

"Hey, kids, you coming down for breakfast?" Aunt Hattie called upstairs to the girls.

There were groaning answers from above, but in a few minutes Ellen appeared in the kitchen. Ellen was the oldest, a senior in high school. "The others'll be down in a few minutes." She followed her father's gaze out the back window. He was waiting for her mother to come home from her job as night nurse in the hospital.

"Here's Nellie!" Her father's tired face lit up as he rose to open the door for his wife. "Hello, darling." He kissed her affectionately. Mrs. Randall sank down on the rocking chair that Aunt Hattie kept in the kitchen. She was obviously worn out. "Was it a rough night?" Mr. Randall poured a cup of coffee for her.

"I'll say it was. Two floor nurses out sick, and the place full up. What a night! But today's the day, isn't it? Where are the girls? Aren't they getting ready for the demonstration?"

"They're coming down in a minute." Ellen spoke for her three little sisters. She looked very much like her mother, with the same dark eyes, light brown skin, and finely chiseled features. But where her mother's face and body were delicate, she was strong, more striking with her taller, slim erectness, and the firm determination of her eyes and chin. Ellen paused a moment, and then added, "I am not going to demonstrate." She made the announcement in a low voice, but her glance traveled anxiously across the faces of the three adults.

Their eyes were all on her. Aunt Hattie opened her mouth to speak and then closed it as Mr. Randall addressed his daughter in his soft voice. "Don't say it with a chip on your shoulder. You don't have to, if you don't want to. But why? Are you against an integrated school?"

"To tell the truth, I don't really care. What difference does it make to me whether the school is black, white, yellow, or pink? I'm a senior and I'd like to be able to finish my last year. I have no complaints."

"But Ellen, you can't just think of yourself!" The tired circles around her mother's eyes gave them an unexpected and startling authority. "You have only one more year to go, but think of the children just starting. What's the good of a new building if the school is going to be run the same as the old one? You know as well as I do they have all kinds of honor programs and special courses at the other school that we haven't got. It isn't right."

"Well, let the P.T.A. fight with the school board

about the curriculum. I don't see why we have to boy-cott the school. What good is that going to do, except make everybody lose a whole year? It doesn't matter so much for the little ones, but for the seniors it's ter-rible." Ellen looked defiantly at her parents and Aunt Hattie.

"Who said anything about losing a year?" Aunt Hattie couldn't contain herself any longer. "Never heard such silly talk in my life! Your father went to see Mr. Monroe yesterday. He and the young man in his office said the school board will have to give in; he said the majority of the people in town will be behind us. But we have to get all the colored folks with us. And I tell you, Ellen Randall, you'd better stop this foolish talk and get right up there on that school lawn and sit down with the rest of us. Here!" She stuck a plate of pancakes under Ellen's nose, her whole body quivering with outrage at the girl's argument.

Ellen took the plate and set it carefully on the kitchen table. With slow, deliberate movements she put a pat of butter on the top cake, and then poured the golden maple syrup over them all, watching the syrup dribble down the sides of the cakes and form a little pool on the plate.

"Well, what have you got to say?" her father asked in a low voice.

Ellen looked up and gave him an unexpected, mischievous little grin. "I thought this was a free country," she said. "If I don't want to demonstrate, I don't think I should."

"There are some things you are not old enough to decide," Aunt Hattie said impatiently. "How is it going to look, if George Randall's oldest daughter is conspicuous by her absence? You have an obligation to your family. Your father is one of the leaders of the Negro people in this town, and I'm pretty well known too, if I must say so myself, and your mother—well, everybody knows your mother and where she stands. What are they going to think, if you stay away?"

The three younger Randall children, Sue seven, Helen five, and the baby Gail, were all in the kitchen now, being fed by Aunt Hattie, their eyes wide, listening to the conversation.

"I don't care what they think, Aunt Hattie." Ellen returned her great-aunt's glare evenly. "Are you telling me to go to the demonstration because of what other people will think? What kind of a hypocrite do you take me for?"

"I think you have to make up your own mind," her father said quietly, before Aunt Hattie had a chance to explode. "But loyalty to your family and to your people is not something to be disregarded lightly. Think it over, Ellen."

"Yes," Mrs. Randall echoed her husband's words,

"think it over, honey." She gave a deep sigh. "These are troubled times, and decisions aren't all that easy to make. I wish you could be spared, but I guess no one can be now. We're all in this together."

It was still early when Ellen finished her breakfast. She slipped out the back door, because she wanted to be alone to think. The Randalls had the corner lot and, compared to the rest of the families on the block, who lived in shabby, run-down two-family houses, they were lucky. Their yard had two trees in it, although no one knew the name of them. Mr. Randall called them back-yard trees, because he said they'd grow through any-thing. Earlier in the summer Mrs. Randall had made an effort to tidy up the yard, to clear out the accumu-lation of broken toys that the little girls refused to part with, and to grow some flowers. But no one, including Mrs. Randall, ever had time to take care of them, and now it was surprising to see bright orange and yellow marigolds blooming among the tall weeds. The sight of the sturdy flowers, gay against the odds and ends of the dank yard, brought an odd lump to Ellen's throat. Beauty struggling in sordidness. That was the way she sometimes felt about her family, her people, and her-self. Her mother was beautiful, a good and gentle nurse, but they all knew that she'd never get any farther than her job on the night shift of the hospital that took care of the colored folks. And her father too. He was a college graduate with a degree in engineering, but he had never been able to get a job in his chosen profession. As a teacher he was stuck in the Negro school at the lowest possible salary the city could get away with.

Ellen resented all these things bitterly, just as much as her parents and Aunt Hattie did, and she knew the Negro people had to fight their way out of it. But why did they have to decide to boycott this particular school now? Weren't there a lot of other places and other things to fight for? Why this school now, in her senior year, when she had everything planned to graduate in June, to enter teacher's college, and soon, soon, as soon as possible, to marry Eugene Ritchie? After going to a broken-down, unpleasant old school for so many years, she had been looking forward to the new building with its big gym and auditorium.

Ellen wandered out of the yard into the street. She felt as though it were Sunday morning instead of an ordinary school day. There were groups of children on the stoops, dressed in their Sunday-best clothes, standing around looking the way children do on Sunday, constricted and self-conscious, neither playing nor going anywhere. Ellen wished she were more in the spirit of the block as she watched the small groups of adults talking intently, women leaning across their windowsills watching, with knowing expectant expressions on their faces. Old Mr. Otis had a smile on his face, instead of his usual scowl, as he set his newspapers out on his stand and swept the front of his store.

"It's a fine day," he called out to Ellen cheerily.

"Yes, it is." These September days were still hot, with a clean, dry heat that seemed as if the sun itself was burning the tips of the leaves a brilliant golden orange. It was too beautiful a day to feel so heavy-hearted, it was a momentous day, a day to be marked down in the history of Thomasville. Ellen wished she were happier about it. But a part of her wanted things to stay the way they were. She didn't want to mix with the white people, and she really dreaded the idea of having those self-confident, cocksure, arrogant boys and girls as classmates. She dreaded winning a fight for an integrated school as much as she hated the thought of losing it. She wished she had been born in another time in history when things were all set and securely arranged, without all this upheaval and pain.

She saw Eugene walking toward her down the block, and she realized she had been waiting for him. She was happy to be there to watch him, with the sun on his head, his long, strong legs walking with such determination. "You in a hurry?" She smiled at him. Each time she saw him she felt shy with love for him, unbelieving that this powerful, vibrant, alive boy was bound to her by a tender and gentle love of his own. How remarkable that they should live on the same street, have gone

31

to the same school, be in the same class, that they should have known each other for so long, and then suddenly have discovered that they had the same dreams, that they never tired of talking to each other, that a smile, a touch of the hand, a glance across a room could convey meanings never to be put into words.

"I'm in a hurry to say good-morning to you. Have you decided anything?" His dark eyes searched her face gravely.

"I've decided I'm not going." Ellen's eyes were anxious. She knew this was not the answer Eugene wanted to hear; it would be so much better if she could go along enthusiastically with the others. But she could not pretend about something this important. She had to be absolutely sure of her feelings, and she was not. "I'm not as good as you are, thinking about race first. I don't want to be a selfish fool, but it does seem silly to me, after all these years of going to an awful school, that we should boycott a good, new one."

"The school building has nothing to do with it," Eugene spoke impatiently. "We've talked about this before; there's no sense in saying it all over again. We don't want an all-Negro school, that's all." His face was hurt.

"Don't be angry with me, just because I don't agree with you!" She and Eugene never had fights. It would be awful, ridiculous and insane, if they got into a fight

32

about this. Bad enough that blacks and whites were fighting, but for them to quarrel between themselves. . . . Ellen felt panicky at the idea. "Why do you want so badly to go to school with white kids?" she asked him abruptly.

"Oh, Ellen, I don't. But I don't want to be told that I can't. Do you see the difference?"

"Of course I see the difference—I understand it all in my head—it's just that . . . well, we don't all have to be the kind to demonstrate, do we?" Ellen felt close to tears.

"No, we don't." Eugene's voice was kinder, and he took her hand in his. "Well, I guess I'd better be going, I've got to get the high-school bunch lined up." He gave her a swift kiss on the cheek, and was off.

Ellen wished it wasn't bright morning at that particular moment. She wanted Eugene to fold her in his arms and hold her close. The whole world seemed to be turning upside down and she was afraid. Afraid and ashamed of her fears. She was afraid of upheaval and demonstrations and fighting, afraid of all the confident young white faces that inhabited the outside world and the world of the other high school. She and Eugene had almost fought already. What might happen to them next?

Ellen dashed back into her own yard, her throat tight with a sob. "Ellen, Ellen." Aunt Hattie was calling her.

She wished she could hide until they all left. It was Sunday in the kitchen. Aunt Hattie, dressed in her black going-to-church dress and her stylish velvet hat, the little girls all crisp and starched, and her parents, bright-eyed in their good clothes. "Are you coming, Ellen?" It was Aunt Hattie who asked the question, but all eyes were on her.

Ellen kept her eyes down. Slowly she shook her head. "No, I'm staying home. I'm going to do some studying, just as if I were in school today." She lifted her head and met their eyes steadily.

Aunt Hattie stomped out of the house furiously. Her mother didn't say anything, but her father put his hand on her arm. "You do what your own conscience tells you to do, Daughter. Study hard, we need good teachers." Ellen smiled at him gratefully, but her heart was filled with remorse as the door closed behind them.

The street outside was filling up with Negro families ready to march to the school and sit down on the lawn, barring the way to those who might still want to go in. They wouldn't prevent anyone from entering, but they would sit there in a solid, stoic line. Ellen could hear a soft voice singing outside, and the other voices, young and old, joined in the integration song, *We Shall Overcome*.

Ellen felt herself go weak with shame—she was being disloyal to her own family, her own people. She was a

34

coward, crouching in the house here, hiding behind —what? She didn't know, she didn't know anything except that suddenly with a fierce burst of indignation she hated the whole system, the hidden, inexplicable thing that had ever made a difference between black and white in the beginning. Why did it ever have to happen?

She opened up her French book and tried to concentrate on the page she was reading. If she really studied hard enough, it would give some meaning to what she was doing. If she was being truly honest, if what she wanted was to finish school and go on to teacher's college, then she had to study. She had to prove to herself that she wasn't being a coward, and she also offered up a silent prayer that nothing and no one would take Eugene away from her.

CHAPTER 3

CARLA was well aware that she was stopping in at her father's office after school in the hope of seeing Adam Blake. She had figured out her timing carefully; she knew he attended lectures at the university in the morning, then he would have lunch, and now at three, he would surely be there.

Carla walked down the familiar, shabby, nondescript streets toward the old, frame building where Mr. Monroe had his office. He had been adamant in refusing to move to the new, modern, red-brick office buildings in the center of town. "My clients feel more comfortable coming here," he said. "They don't like fancy fronts. They'd be worried to death that the higher rent would make their bills bigger, as it certainly would." Carla was fascinated by these old streets with their crazy mixture of architecture, each building with a personality of its own, in contrast to the rows of steel and glass on the new streets. Some of the buildings had dates engraved on their weathered brick fronts, 1860, 1867, with stone watering troughs for the horses still standing by the curb. Carla liked to think of the ladies driving up in their carriages, dressed in their long skirts and bustles, stopping to take care of their business and perhaps having a cup of chocolate at the old fashioned ice-cream parlor, which claimed to have been established in 1865 and looked as if it probably had been, with its Victorian iron and marble ice-cream tables and grilled iron chairs.

She was not very far from her own house, when she heard voices singing and saw a number of policemen around. "What's going on?" she asked one of the men in uniform.

"It's the demonstration, over at the colored school," he told her.

"Oh." It was a couple of blocks out of her way, but Carla decided she wanted to see it. She had read about similar demonstrations in the newspaper, but she had never actually seen one, and now, right here in Thomasville, one was taking place, just a short distance from her father's office and where she lived!

There seemed to be more people on the streets than usual as she hurried toward the school, in the direction of the singing, and Carla thought the people, the white people, had rather sheepish expressions on their faces. One red-faced man walked by glaring at everyone, muttering that these things should be stopped. The people

37

who heard him laughed uneasily, but didn't say anything.

Carla felt a surge of excitement as the singing got
louder, and when she turned the corner and saw the
double line of dark-skinned people walking up and
down in front of the school, she felt an unexpected
lump in her throat. They were a most impressive sight.
Although mostly women and children, there were some
men too, and whole families seemed to have turned out,
young women pushing baby carriages, and some carry-
ing children in their arms. The singing swelled to an
end on one clear note, and then the demonstrators
walked quietly. There were women of all ages, grand-
mothers walking with daughters and tots, some well-
dressed, others shabbily with bare legs and torn shoes,
and yet all of them flowed together in one unified
whole. The placards that they carried touched Carla
so that her eyes filled up; they were so obviously ama-
teurish, painstakingly handmade. She could almost see
heads bent over kitchen tables laboriously lettering
them: *A New School, But the Same Old Segregation!
We Do Not Want a Separate School! Double Schools
Cost Money—We Don't Want Them!*

Some of the older women had brought chairs and
were sitting on the new lawn right in front of the
empty, dark brick building. They looked at ease and
comfortable, as if they could and would sit there for-

ever until they got their way. Timidly, Carla walked up a little closer to the line of marchers. She recognized a couple of the white ministers in town, and then she saw Hattie, walking at the head of the line, dressed in black, her head held high. Carla didn't know what to do; she didn't know whether to go over and talk to her, whether to wave to her, or what. She felt foolish, almost like a curiosity seeker standing there watching them, but then Hattie spied her and gave her a big friendly smile and waved hello to her. Carla waved back. She wondered if she should join them, should walk around with them, but she was too shy. There should be some of us from our high school walking with them, she thought. We should be there with them if they want us. Hattie did not stop to talk, she just waved and smiled and walked on.

Carla became acutely aware of her own exclusion. Suddenly she felt uncomfortable and ashamed. Here was this tremendous thing taking place in her own city, part of something big and deeply important that was happening all over the country, and she was only an onlooker.

Carla hurried on to her father's office. He would have some ideas, he would know what to do.

She found him deep in discussion with Adam when she arrived, and she was hesitant about interrupting them. "It's all right, come on in." Her father motioned her to sit down. His eyes scanned her, glancing at her new cotton knit, her hair pinned up instead of hanging loose, but she felt he wasn't really looking at her at all. He had a preoccupied frown between his eyes while he paced around the office like a caged animal.

"I just walked by the demonstration at the school," Carla said excitedly. "It's terrific, absolutely terrific. It's so moving . . . they all look so, I don't know, so dignified and purposeful. Have you seen them?" she asked her father.

"No, I've been too busy. Demonstrations are all right, but they need a lot more than a bunch of women and kids parading in front of a school. We need some action in this town!"

"If you saw them you wouldn't think it was nothing." Carla was hurt by her father's quick dismissal of the demonstration. She had been genuinely moved and excited by it, and wanted to talk about finding a way to participate, to become a part of the drama that was taking place.

"Your father's had a rough day," Adam said with a wry smile. "He's got a lot on his mind."

"So it seems." Carla looked at her father inquiringly. He was always involved in his own affairs, she thought, both admiring and envying the passion with which he approached everything he did, and resenting it too. He was dynamic and energetic, but bound up within himself.

"The Mayor is setting up a commission to present plans to clear the city of slums and segregation." Mr. Monroe walked over to a map of the city on his wall and pointed to a red encircled area. Carla knew it well, a wasteland of old tenements and empty city warehouses along the river. "The most naturally beautiful part of our city is just a dump!" Her father had a visionary look in his eyes. "We're going to turn it into something to be proud of, good homes, playgrounds, parks, maybe even a marina for small boats. A place where people, black and white, can live and enjoy living." His eyes were glowing as he turned back to Carla and Adam. "It's going to be the greatest thing the city ever did."

"It sounds wonderful. But what's it got to do with you?" Carla asked her father.

He grinned. "The Mayor wants me to head up the commission." He spoke in an offhand way, but Carla knew her father well enough to tell that he was intensely excited about the proposal and that now nothing else would occupy his mind.

She felt a glow of pride in him. "Oh, Daddy, that's terrific! You're going to do it, of course."

"I haven't decided yet. It means we'd have to tighten up, Carla. I'd be taking a big cut in income, the job doesn't pay much. Adam could carry on here some, but I'd have to put aside much of my law practice. I have to give the matter a lot of thought."

"I'll do everything I can, sir," Adam put in.

Mr. Monroe looked at the younger man affectionately. "I couldn't think of doing it without you, Adam."

"But you must do it!" Her father was within arm's reach and impulsively Carla stretched out her hand to pat his shoulder. She was surprised and moved when he pressed her hand for a few seconds. He had a happy, boyish look on his face that made Carla suddenly wonder if his standoffishness was only a defense. It seemed ridiculous to think of her father as being shy, he was so self-confident and assured, and yet. . . . Carla tucked away the thought to ponder over later.

"Well, it means a lot of thankless work and plenty of headaches. I'll have to think about it," he repeated. Carla was sure he didn't mean a word he was saying. Her father would never turn down a chance like this, to work at something so close to his heart and that he believed in so thoroughly. His excitement made her feel her own exclusion even more keenly. She felt let down, as if everyone in the world had a purpose except herself. "You'll do it," she said to him, wishing she could forget herself in his enthusiasm.

"Of course he will." Adam's eyes on her were

42

sympathetic. "Want to go down for coffee? I'd like to hear some more about the demonstration."

Carla's face lit up. "I'd love some coffee. You coming, Dad?"

"No, I have work to do. You two go along."

Carla was grateful for Adam's interest. He is sensitive and perceptive, she thought, as she sat opposite him in the old fashioned ice-cream parlor across the street. She spoke to him eagerly about the demonstration, and then, shyly, she tried to tell him some of the things that she was feeling. "It was so funny seeing Hattie there. I never would have thought of her leading a march, she always seemed so proper and conservative. I never really thought about her color, and I'm sure my mother never did, but I guess it was on her mind all the time. It made me feel kind of ashamed, seeing her there." Carla sighed. "I wish I could do something. I feel out of it all."

"I know." Adam's eyes were understanding. "I know what you mean. You could join the demonstration, walk along with them, couldn't you?"

"Yes, I could do that." Carla was ashamed to say that she had been too shy to do even that. "But I'd like to do something more, well, something more specific than that."

"We all would," Adam said soberly, "but some of us have to wait for the chance. It'll be great if your father

43

takes that job. It must be wonderful having Mr. Monroe for a father," Adam said unexpectedly.

"It certainly is." Carla felt a great rapport between herself and Adam. Adam had the habit of nodding his head while listening, holding it to one side, making her feel that he was completely absorbed in what she had to say. "He's lucky to have you in the office now," she added shyly.

Adam laughed. "I'm the one who's lucky. I can learn a lot from a man like Mr. Monroe." Then he added with his quick smile, "I could sit here talking for hours, but I'd better be getting back to work."

"Me too. I think I will join the demonstration, it's a good idea."

"I'm glad."

When Carla left Adam, she crossed to the shady side of the street and walked slowly, not stopping to look in the shop windows, but lost in her own thoughts. She wondered if she were falling in love. Was it possible to fall in love with someone you'd only seen twice in your life, and knew so little about? But what do you have to know about someone to fall in love . . . wasn't it really yourself and your own feelings that you had to know best? Carla *felt* different when she was with Adam, although she didn't know how to describe the feeling. She felt smooth and serene and yet excited at the same time. It was a good feeling and gave her a new awareness of everything, even the motion of her body as she walked toward home. She felt gloriously glad to be alive, to be seventeen, to be almost beautiful.

Crossing Hawthorne Avenue and Main Street, Carla suddenly remembered that in her eagerness to see Adam she had completely forgotten her books. It was an awful nuisance going all the way back to school now, but she had to have her books to do her homework.

At least she could save some time by taking a bus back to school.

Much to her surprise, Carla found a group of her friends sitting on the lawn in front of the school. "What's up?" she asked, sinking down on the grass beside Gadge.

"We are having a, quote, serious discussion, close quote," Gadge said.

"It *is* serious," Twinkey emphasized. She moved to make more room for Carla. Everyone said Twinkey was going to be stunning when she grew up. Now she was too plump, but she had good legs and shoulders, a gay face, and it wasn't hard to imagine her as a very handsome young woman.

Mary Jane Peterson, Fred Dingee, and Chris and Gail Waters made up the rest of the group. "We're talking about the boycott of the new school, the one that's down near you," Fred told her.

"I saw them picketing this afternoon," Carla said

45

excitedly. "It's terrific. I wish we could do something about it. Help in some way."

"That's what we've been talking about. We want to get in on the act, but we don't know how," Gadge said.

"I don't see why we can't go and join the demonstration. That will show our support." Twinkey looked around the circle of faces.

"We can," Chris and Gail spoke together, and Carla nodded her head. Gail always agreed with everything her older brother said.

"Yes, we can," Gadge repeated, "but it seems to me we could do something more than that. The whole thing is so cockeyed. Of the seven of us here, four of us should really be going to that new school instead of traveling all across the city every day. Think of all the money that has been spent on school buses over the years just getting us to school. It's nutty."

"Well, why don't we go to the new school?" Carla's eyes were wide with surprise at the startling simplicity of her suggestion. "Why don't we just go?"

Carla spoke into the sudden dead silence. "The school board couldn't reasonably object. As Gadge said, think of the money they'd save on transportation. And if the white kids in the neighborhood went to the school, it would automatically be integrated. We could be the ones to start. The four of us." Her glance took in Gadge, Twinkey, and Mary Jane.

46

Gadge was the first to speak. "That's the best idea I've heard yet. Why didn't I think of that! We could have done it years ago."

"We wouldn't have wanted to, not in that horrible old building they used to have. But now with a new school it makes sense. Except, I don't know, I'd be a little scared." Twinkey's round face was solemn.

"What's there to be scared of? You think all those kids run around with switchblades or knives?" Gadge asked mockingly.

"Some of them do," Twinkey said. "And to change now in our senior year. . . . I love Mr. Martin in French, I'd hate to give him up."

"Me too," Carla said. "We don't know what kind of teachers they have over there or anything."

"It was your idea, don't back out now!" Gadge looked at Carla accusingly.

"I'm not backing out. But we have to be sensible. We don't want to go off half-cocked."

"Well there was nothing sensible about going way across town all these years to Lincoln. Maybe we should stop worrying about being sensible and do something dramatic." Gadge's light eyes were sparkling.

"We'd have to get permission to change." Mary Jane had been quiet up until now. "I don't know if my parents will let me." Mary Jane's parents were traditional

47

Southerners, and no one wanted to discuss how they might feel about it.

"Well, we can try, can't we?" Gadge stood up, stretching his thin legs. "Let's ask our parents, and meet tomorrow afternoon after school. Then we can take it from there. O.K.?"

Everyone agreed. The group also discovered how late it was and started to hurry home. Carla went inside to get her books and found Gadge waiting for her when she came out. They fell into step together.

"Do you think it will really make any difference, a few of us switching schools?" Carla wondered aloud.

"Every little thing makes a difference. It doesn't seem like much, nothing does by itself, but it all adds up. Are you sorry you made the suggestion?"

"It sounded so simple at first, but now it seems like a futile gesture and more complicated. What good can it do anybody?"

"It may be only a token, but I think it will mean a lot to the kids going to that school. It will make them feel that at least some of the people in the neighborhood think the same way they do, and don't believe in segregation. That's important."

"I suppose so." They walked in silence for a few blocks. Then Carla asked, "What'll we do? How do we go about switching schools?"

"After we get our parents' permission, I guess we

should go to the principal, Mr. Casey, and I suppose he has to ask the school board. I don't know, I've never done anything like this before."

"Me either, but it's exciting." Carla felt a wave of anticipation and excitement flood through her. She thought of Hattie's face, and the rows of sober, dark-skinned faces singing. . . . It would be tremendous to be really part of their fight, to *do* something!

That night Mr. Monroe ate his dinner hurriedly and was eager to go off to a meeting, but while they were eating, Carla told him of their plan. "Sounds like a good idea. Don't know how much it will accomplish, but it's a step in the right direction."

Dan was more enthusiastic. "It's a great idea. I'm for it. What do we do, when do we start?"

"That's what I wanted to ask you about," Carla addressed her father. "What do you think we should do?"

"The first thing is to get the support of the school, see how many parents agree. Maybe you could send some letters home to the parents. You'd better get the principal's backing before you do anything. Then if you get a good response, someone will have to go to the school board and get their approval. I think you should discuss your plans with the leaders of the boycott of the Negro school. You'll want to work along with them. It will help their case to know that some of the white students want to switch schools."

"But that sounds as if it's going to take forever," Carla wailed.

"Not forever, but it all takes time." Mr. Monroe drank down his coffee and left the table.

When Dan had gone upstairs to do his homework, Carla sat near the telephone. She wished she had the courage to call up Adam; she'd love to be able to talk to him about their plans. She was sure he would give his attention and help, but she didn't have the nerve to call him.

CHAPTER 4

THE social room attached to the Negro Baptist Church was filled with people. At one end, seated at a long table, were the leaders of the community, the minister, the head of the NAACP, some professional men and businessmen, Aunt Hattie representing the Women's Auxiliary, and Eugene representing the high school. The others, men, women, and children, were grouped around on folding chairs. They were having a meeting to report on what had been accomplished up to date on the week-old boycotting of the new school, and to make plans for what to do next.

Ellen sat next to her father, each of them holding a sleepy little girl, with Sue, the seven-year-old, on the other side of Ellen, trying hard to keep awake. It was evening, and Mrs. Randall was in the hospital at work. Ellen's eyes were glued on Eugene. It had been a trying week for them. Ellen had kept her vow of studying hard so that when the school opened again she wouldn't be too far behind, but she felt she hadn't done a very good job. Her mind wasn't on history and algebra and

French. There had been too much going on, too much excitement in the air, and she was worried about what was happening between her and Eugene. He had been busy with the demonstrations and meetings, and while he had pointedly not asked her to join in the marching, she knew that he was impatient with her for not doing so. And she was getting uneasy with herself. In a way, she was sorry she had taken the stand she had, and although her feeling about the boycott hadn't really changed, she hated the idea that she wasn't doing her share and that she was being left out. Now that the demonstrations were an accomplished fact, it seemed foolish of her not to join in, but she wanted Eugene to ask her. She realized she had boxed herself in. Eugene wanted her to take the initiative, and she wanted Eugene to make it easy for her and try to persuade her to join in again. As a result, nothing was happening. Although the situation disturbed her, she didn't know how to change it.

Eugene was reporting now on the high-school turnout. He looked so handsome and so vibrant standing and addressing the group, Ellen wished she was there beside him. Her mother had made a few remarks to her on Sunday that she kept remembering. "Things are going to be different for you," Mrs. Randall had said. "Maybe our Negro men aren't going to be so beaten anymore; they're going to stand up for themselves. Be glad your Eugene isn't afraid to go after what is coming to him. Don't hold him back, Ellen. Our men have been taking a licking for too long; they need their women to stand up with them now, not to be scared anymore." That's all her mother had said, but her words had hit home.

Eugene sat down now, and the principal of the school began to speak. He was suggesting a plan for tutoring the elementary grades during the school boycott. Ellen sat up straight in her chair, shifting little Gail in her arms. "We need help," he was saying, "for the lower grades. Some of our regular staff is available, but we would like to break up the classes into smaller groups. Perhaps some of the high-school students would volunteer to take classes?" He looked around the audience inquiringly.

Ellen, too, gave a swift glance around the room. The girls and boys there from the high school were each looking to see what the others were doing, but no one raised his hand. It didn't take Ellen long to make up her mind. Impulsively her hand shot up, and she spoke in her clear, low voice. "I would be glad to do some tutoring." Immediately several other hands went up, and the principal with a pleased smile on his face jotted down their names. "That's fine, just fine. . . . Will you please all stay after the meeting, so we can get together and make arrangements."

53

Mr. Randall leaned across to Ellen and patted her arm. "That was a good thing to do, I'm proud of you."

"It's nothing very much, but I like it better than marching with everyone staring at me. I'm glad I'll have a chance to do something," she added.

She was much more elated than she cared to show. The idea of tutoring the small children came as something made-to-order for her. She really loved teaching and children, and it was as if a great weight had been lifted from her. Eugene's eyes were on her, and she looked back at him with a smile. There was no mistaking his delight in what she had just done. Aunt Hattie was beaming at her, and Ellen relaxed for the first time all week. Now she could look around the room without feeling like a leper. "We each have to find our place in this movement," her father whispered. "We can't all do the same things." Ellen nodded her agreement.

Ellen noticed Aunt Hattie's eyes turning to the door frequently, and she wondered whom she was expecting. She didn't have long to wait. In a few minutes the door opened and a young girl and boy came in, both white. They hesitated, but Aunt Hattie stood up and waved a greeting to them, calling to them to come on in. Aunt Hattie introduced them to the audience by name, Carla Monroe and Gadge Conefry. "They have something very important to tell this meeting, and I invited them to come." Aunt Hattie turned to the two. "Would one of you like to tell them what you're planning, please?"

The boy named Gadge stepped forward, and Ellen couldn't help but smile to herself at the relief on the girl's face. She was the daughter of the people Aunt Hattie worked for. A pretty girl, Ellen thought, in a pale way. She liked the boy's face as he addressed the group. His voice was a little nervous, but he spoke clearly. "There isn't very much to tell you," he said, "but a bunch of us in Lincoln High School who live nearby have decided that we would like to switch over to River High School. When it's open again," he added with a grin. "We have our parents' approval, and our principal says he won't stand in our way, so we thought that whenever you plan to meet with the Board of Education, maybe one of us could go along and be spokesman for our group."

Ellen could barely hear him because of the loud burst of applause that greeted his words. The boy looked startled and happy at the great enthusiasm. Everyone at the table stood up and shook hands with him and with Carla, and then Aunt Hattie asked them to sit down. Aunt Hattie said a few words, thanking them for the wonderful support this request would give them in dealing with the Board of Education, and the meeting was over.

Eugene rushed over to Ellen and picked up Gail in

his arms. "I'll carry her," he offered. "But I'd like to talk to those kids from Lincoln High." The two white faces, however, had gone. "Too bad," Eugene murmured. "I'm sorry they left so soon."

"I'm not exactly sorry," Ellen said, gathering up the children's jackets and helping her father put them on without waking up the girls completely. Eugene didn't answer her, but Ellen suspected he would later.

In a few minutes Aunt Hattie came along and said she would take the children home with Mr. Randall. "You two don't have to bother," she told Ellen and Eugene. "You have to wait for that meeting here, Ellen, but don't stay out late. I'm glad you're doing that tutoring." Aunt Hattie looked very pleased with herself. "How do you like those kids? I've been telling you they're good kids. Imagine their coming here to say they want to switch schools! How about that!" She was clucking like a pleased mother hen.

The arrangements for the tutoring didn't take long to make, and soon Ellen and Eugene were outside. Eugene suggested a Coke, and they walked over to the corner drugstore. When they were seated at a table, Eugene turned sideways to look at Ellen, who was beside him. "That was great about the tutoring. For a minute I didn't think anyone was going to volunteer. I'm glad you started it."

Ellen shrugged. "I wanted to do something."

Eugene squeezed her arm. "I know. But what was that crack about those white kids? You didn't sound very happy about their coming!"

"I knew you wouldn't let that go by." Ellen smiled, but she was still worried about herself and Eugene. Was all this race business going to split them apart? "I didn't mind their coming," she spoke slowly, trying to find her words, "but I don't like making such a big thing of it. I didn't feel like going up to them and giving them a pat on the back for the great deed they're doing. So they're switching to a school in their neighborhood, so what? What's so great about that?"

"Sometimes you really get me mad," Eugene said with exasperation. "One minute you're with it, like offering to tutor, and the next minute you pull something like this. Honey, we need the whites in this fight. We need everyone, and don't keep looking a gift horse in the mouth. Whatever they do is a help to us!"

Ellen sat up straight, moving away from Eugene. "Now you listen to me. I'm sick of your acting so high and mighty, thinking you know all the answers. Every time I disagree with you, you act as if there's something wrong with me! I don't want anything to do with those white kids, and if you do, that's your business, but I don't have to think they're wonderful." Her face was strained with indignation, but her eyes, searching Eugene's face, were anxious. She had thought that the

57

tensions between them would be eased, now that she was going to tutor (although that was not why she was doing it), but she saw that they were still there, and her frustration came out in anger.

Eugene's face was grave. "I guess we don't agree," he said unhappily. "I think things are only going to change if everyone works together. You think it's only our job. But that's no reason for us to fight."

"I don't want to fight," Ellen said glumly. She turned around to Eugene impulsively. "This whole business scares me. I almost wish things would go along as they were, if it makes us fight and keeps us out of school all year. . . ." She was sorry she had said the words out loud, they sounded so weak.

Eugene shook his head sadly. "You shouldn't think like that Ellen, you shouldn't." But he put his arm around her in protection, as if he wanted to stand between her and all the hardships that they were both facing and would still have to face. Gratefully Ellen put her head on his shoulder, happy to count on his strength to help her through.

It was noticeably beginning to get dark earlier, and in the dry October afternoons the women along River Street were raking up the leaves. They stopped to talk to each other and to look toward the river, trying to catch a glimpse of the blue water between the ugly, abandoned warehouses. Some of the women sat on their stoop while their children raked the leaves into neat piles, carefully covering each pile with twigs to keep the leaves from blowing away. The women talked about their children, about the high prices in the food market, what the meat specials were for the week, and how they'd better be ordering coal for the winter. It was the comfortable, female talk of women who have lived side by side watching each other's children grow, knowing the details of each other's lives. They had the intimacy of a close-knit neighborhood, forced by circumstances to be sufficient unto itself, cut off from the mainstream of the city.

In the Baptist church Ellen had her eyes on the clock. She wasn't waiting for three o'clock to come around, so she could dismiss the third graders whom she had been teaching. The teaching hours did not drag by for her. But today she had started watching the clock right after lunch at one; this was the big day of the meeting with the Board of Education. Proposals had been sent to the board covering the demands of the Negro community. Their ultimate goal was to desegregate the two schools completely, with the Lincoln school building taking in the first six grades and the new River school becoming the junior and senior high school. But compromises had been discussed, and interim steps proposed, including the immediate transfer of some white students to River and some Negro students to Lincoln. Today a committee of both Negroes and whites were meeting with the Board of Education, and they hoped to come out with a final decision.

The meeting was set for one-thirty. Eugene was going to be there, and the boy, Gadge, who had spoken at the church, was representing the white students. It was hard for Ellen to keep her mind on the arithmetic and spelling, it kept wandering to the grimy building downtown, where the Superintendent of Schools had his office and where the meeting was being held.

Before the afternoon was over, they would know the outcome. This might be the last class she would have with her children. Ellen looked over the group affectionately. She would miss the girls in their little starched dresses, the wide-eyed boys, ready for mischief but eager to learn, all of them bright and still excited about this new way of coming to school in the church, having a small class and a high-school girl for a teacher.

Ellen closed her spelling book. "We're going to draw pictures now," she said, and smiled at the joyous reception her announcement received. In a few minutes she had two small boys handing out paper and crayons. "How about making pictures of the new school? Just draw it the way it looks to you." Ellen walked among her small group to watch what they were doing, but every few minutes her eyes went back to the clock. It was after two now . . . soon it would be two-thirty. Supposing the meeting went on for two hours, that would take it up to three-thirty; it would be four o'clock before Eugene would get across town to bring the word. Ellen tried to keep her attention on the entertaining versions of the new red-brick building emerging on the children's drawing paper.

At five minutes to three Ellen collected the papers. The children were coming up to say good-bye to her when the door burst open and Eugene came in. "School's going to open Monday," he announced breathlessly.

A cry went up from the children. Ellen wasn't sure whether it was one of joy or sorrow. She was dying to hear Eugene's news, but she turned to her group first. "Are you glad?" she asked them with a grin.

"No, no, no," they chorused. "We like you to teach us."

"I'm glad," one little girl said. "I want to go back to school."

"We all want to go back to school," Ellen said. "You'll be very happy there." Since it was Friday, Ellen realized this class had been her last. "I guess we'll have to say good-bye," she said. "I'll come visit you in school." She bent down and kissed each of them as they came up one by one to say good-bye.

The minute the children were gone Ellen turned to

Eugene. "What happened? Tell me everything. We must have won if the school's opening! Oh, Eugene, it is wonderful, isn't it?" She stepped up close to him so that they could hug each other. Ellen felt the excitement of victory in her blood . . . all the painful weeks, now it was over and *they had won!*

"Well, we didn't win everything." Eugene looked at her uncertainly. "Knowing you, you won't think it's so much, but remember it's only a beginning. I don't know how it would have turned out if those kids hadn't offered to transfer. Anyway ten high-school students from River will be transferred to Lincoln, and ten from Lincoln will come to us. It's only a pilot program for this school year. Starting next September they'll begin integrating the elementary grades and do more with the high-school students—they want to work out the geography of who goes where. But they wouldn't discuss separating the elementary and high schools yet. There are a lot of plans in the works, and a third school will probably be built that will change everything."

"You mean just ten kids are being switched?" Ellen's disappointment showed on her face. "And you settled for that?"

"We had to." Eugene's lips were set in a determined line. "If you had been there you'd understand. There are so many complicated problems about transportation, and the budget has been set for this year. I think the board was sincere, I think they're really trying, and we have to give them a chance. When you sit face to face with them, you know that everything can't be done overnight!"

"They've had years to do it in," Ellen said drily. "Oh, Eugene, I thought we'd really won something!"

"We have. All of us who were there felt we won. I hope everyone else doesn't take it the way you do," he added morosely.

"Well, I can't really get excited about it." Ellen looked at him unhappily. "But I'll try," she added with a little smile. "I'm sure you did your best."

"You can really get me angry! First you didn't want to demonstrate, and now you're not satisfied with what we've done." Eugene picked up the children's drawings and glanced through them.

"Please don't be angry with me." Ellen plucked at his sleeve, her eyes pleading. "These are awful days, and sometimes I get scared and I don't know what I want. I know I switch back and forth! I couldn't demonstrate, because I couldn't bear all those people staring at me; I'm scared even of ten white kids coming to our school. I've never been to a white kid's house, I've never been to a dance with white kids. You know me, I even hate to go downtown to their big stores. The saleswomen don't like to wait on a colored girl. They always bring her something gaudy and awful, and if she wants to try on something decent, they say they haven't got it in her size. We get insulted right and left, and yet you say we've got to be friends, we've got to take their little handouts and their promises."

Eugene swung around and took her in his arms. "You don't have to tell me about it. But it *is* different now. Now we're not taking their handouts, we're *fighting* for what we want. That makes a big difference."

Ellen clung to him tightly. Eugene was her only anchor in this topsy-turvy world. They held to each other with a painful intensity, willing their differences to vanish in their physical embrace, but Ellen knew with an intuitive foreboding that they were going to have to make more and more adjustments in the days ahead.

"Come on, let's go out," Eugene suggested.

Ellen looked at the pile of drawings, the papers, and the few books she had been using with the children on the desk she had improvised from a table. "I don't know what to do with these. I guess I'll leave them here for now." Impulsively she went through the drawings quickly and picked out a few. "I'm going to keep these," she said, putting them carefully into her briefcase.

Eugene smiled affectionately at her sentimentality.

The news had already spread, and a group of women and children were in front of the church. Everyone seemed to be talking at once, and Ellen gathered from the snatches of conversation she heard that there were many differences of opinion as to how much of a victory they had won. In hearing some of the criticism, Ellen felt a loyalty to Eugene; he had been one of perhaps a dozen people working the hardest and should be supported now. It was easy to stand on the sidelines and criticize, and Ellen felt ashamed of her own behavior.

Eugene headed Ellen down to the river, past the old warehouses. "There's talk about all these old buildings coming down," he said. "Boy, wouldn't I love to design the new ones. What a marvelous job could be done with this riverfront." Eugene had a glowing, visionary look in his eyes. "This could be the most exciting part of the city."

Ellen looked at him with pride, but she thought to herself, What chance has he got of ever doing it? A little colored boy wanting to design a new city! "Maybe someday you'll design a building," she said, trying to sound convincing. "Maybe you'll build a house for us."

"Oh, I'll do that," Eugene said confidently. "But to take a place like this and turn it into something, that would be a real achievement. I'd have a park here by the water, and the buildings set back. . . . I think they could be designed so that almost every apartment had a view. And I'd make use of the roofs, the way some apartment buildings in France were designed. I saw pictures of them in a magazine. . . ."

Ellen was entranced listening to Eugene and watching his face. He was so sure of himself, so excited and exciting. He wanted more than anything in the world to be an architect, and she thought maybe he could do it, maybe he could really do it. Her love for him almost hurt she felt it so sharply. Eugene was right when he said that today was just a beginning, and yet as they walked through the shabby streets and past the dump lots, she wished desperately that she could protect him from setting his sights too high. Would he ever be happy as a school teacher, living the way their parents lived? Ellen clung to his arm, listening with both pain and joy as he unfolded his vision of a beautiful city to her.

When they came back to the church they found preparations under way for a big meeting that night. "To celebrate our victory," Aunt Hattie announced as she met them. There was a festive, excited feeling in the air, and the consensus was that the Negro community had won a victory. The spirit was contagious and Ellen and Eugene joined the other young people in decorating the hall where a full report would be made that night, and, later, a little celebration party would be held.

CHAPTER 5

CARLA set the timer for ten minutes, and carefully dropped three eggs into the water to boil, two for Dan and one for herself. Her father hated boiled eggs, even hard ones, and preferred to cook his own. Breakfast was the only meal he was fussy about, making a great to-do about having his juice not too warm and not too cold, the toast exactly the right color, the butter easy to spread, his scrambled eggs soft but not runny, and his coffee very hot and very strong.

"It's nice not having to rush to make the bus," Carla said to Dan, putting a large mound of mayonnaise on his plate for his egg.

"It's the only good part about this whole thing." Dan drank his orange juice down in one gulp.

"Don't say that. The whole thing is good and important."

"It all seems kind of silly to me. What's been accomplished? So a few of us are changing to River High, and a few Negro kids are going to Lincoln, but both schools are really still separate. It's just a token gesture."

"Well the Negroes seem to think it's important. They had a celebration Friday night."

"It's sad to think they had to celebrate over this," Dan said. "It's the saddest thing I ever heard of."

"They don't want you feeling sorry for them, that's for sure. Lots of small things are important that we never think about. How many years has Hattie been working for us? I guess a few years before I was born, so it's over seventeen, and all those years she's been coming around the back to the kitchen door. Saturday, when she came to work, she came in the front door, and I could tell by the look on her face she had done something important. As if she couldn't have come in the front door all the time! Neither one of us said anything, but it made me sick thinking about it. Imagine, wanting to come in the front door and not doing it for almost twenty years!"

Dan shook his head woefully.

Mr. Monroe came into the kitchen with his quick, impatient stride. "Aren't you two kids late today?"

"We're walking to school, remember? We don't have to take the bus."

"Oh, yes, of course. Today's your first day at the new school. Well, lots of luck. Hope everything goes smoothly."

"Don't worry, it will. It'll be just as dull as any other

68

day at school. No chance of some excitement." Dan sounded regretful.

"There are certain kinds of excitement we can happily do without." Mr. Monroe was dropping his eggs into a bowl and concentrating on beating them.

Carla moved rapidly out of his way. Until her father had his breakfast she preferred to stay as far from him as possible. Her only run-ins with him occurred before breakfast when his temper was at the surface, ready to pop off. He had been very preoccupied lately, and Carla wondered what was worrying him. She had a feeling that when she and Dan spoke to him he wasn't really listening, which wasn't like him. Usually he concentrated on whatever was happening at that minute, no matter how small it was, giving every word, every detail, his utmost attention.

"Wonder what kind of a football coach the school has," Dan said. "River's got a pretty good team. They have some big fellows there. I guess I won't stand a chance."

No one answered Dan. Carla was wondering how she could unobtrusively bring Adam's name up. She was dying to know how he was doing in her father's office, but she didn't know how to ask. Mr. Monroe had finished scrambling his eggs, his toast was done, and he was sitting down to eat. It always struck Carla as funny to see her father fuss so much about his breakfast, and then wolf it down in five minutes. Why all that bother when it was gone so quickly?

"Well, Dan, come on. I guess we'd better be going." Carla's feelings were mixed about the new school. She was curious to see what it was like, but she also felt nervous and apprehensive. She was glad that Twinkey and Gadge were going to be there too. Mary Jane's parents had flatly refused to let her change schools, and the Board of Education had not encouraged anyone to change who didn't want to. Carla had heard that only ten white students were coming to River.

Carla's heart sank when she said good-bye to Dan at the school entrance. "Good luck," she called after him. Somehow she had missed meeting Gadge and Twinkey, and now, leaving Dan and realizing she had to walk into a strange classroom alone, she had a terrible case of jitters. She wondered why she had ever let herself get into this situation, why she had been so willing to switch schools in her senior year. As Dan had said the whole thing was a token gesture, and what was she really accomplishing? She wasn't going to change the world, or even change anything much in Thomasville. Carla felt that if she were going to make a sacrifice it should be for something big and important, something more dramatic than walking a few blocks to a school.

Small groups of boys and girls were standing in the

classroom when Carla entered. She looked around at them and realized with a start that she was the only white person in the room. Evidently Twinkey and Gadge hadn't arrived yet, or perhaps they were in another class; the three of them were the only senior transfers from Lincoln High. The teacher, an attractive dark-skinned young woman, busy at her desk, looked up and nodded a greeting to Carla. Carla stood uncertainly in the doorway, not knowing what to do with herself. She wished she could flee out of the room, out of the building. This must be the way *they* feel, she thought. Oh, if Twinkey or Gadge would only come along!

A tall, dark, very handsome boy stepped away from the others and came over to her, holding out his hand. She recognized him as the boy who had been at the church meeting. "I'm Eugene Ritchie," he said to her. "I'm acting president of the class until we have an election this year. We're glad to see you here."

Gratefully Carla shook hands with him. "I'm glad to be here." She smiled at him shyly. "I'm sorry there aren't more of us," she added.

"We're sorry too. But we're grateful that some of you didn't mind changing."

"It isn't much. It's easier for us, because we live so nearby. It's much nicer than taking the bus."

71

Eugene laughed. "Well, lots of us wouldn't mind riding that bus over to Lincoln High."

Carla blushed; she had put her foot right into it! "Yes, of course, I know," she stammered.

"Come on and meet some of the crowd." Eugene's eyes were friendly. He introduced her to a group of boys and girls, but he said the names too quickly for her to grasp them, and Carla was too uncomfortable and shy to ask him to repeat them. The only name she recognized was Ellen Randall, whom she had seen fleetingly a few times in the past.

"You're Hattie's niece, aren't you?" Carla asked.

"Yes." Ellen's face was a cool mask. "Mrs. Randall is my great-aunt," she said, in a tone of voice that made Carla want to shrivel up and disappear.

Carla blushed again, furiously, wanting to fall through the floor. It would be ridiculous to call Hattie Mrs. Randall, she thought, after she had called her Hattie for years. Why, Hattie is like one of the family. . . . Ellen must hate me, Carla thought, and she felt her own embarrassment and uneasiness turn into anger. She has no right hating me. I've never done anything to her, and it isn't my fault that her great-aunt took a job years ago working for my mother! It's a good job, too, and Hattie, her Mrs. Randall, seems to be happy with it. No one's forcing her to work for us, she gets well paid. . . .

Ellen turned to someone else in the group. Then Twinkey and Gadge arrived, and Eugene introduced them around. A bell rang through the building, and they were told to take seats. Carla, Twinkey, and Gadge had decided beforehand that they would not sit together, so they all went off in different directions. In the confusion of getting seated, Carla to her dismay found herself sitting right next to Ellen. Carla was at the end of the row, so that the only one she could possibly talk to would be Ellen. Just my luck, Carla thought woefully.

Carla looked around the room the first chance she had. Aside from herself and her two friends, the class was completely dark-skinned. It was odd, Carla thought, she felt in the middle of a situation that was backwards. Every day in the newspapers there were stories of Negro children entering predominantly white schools, and she thought of the feelings of the Negro boys and girls who were spending their first day at Lincoln. But what about the white kids who were going to the almost all-colored schools? Why didn't the newspapermen ever write about them?

She knew the answer her father would have. He'd say you have the choice, but they don't and that's what makes the difference. It was true. She didn't *have* to go to this school, and neither did Gadge nor Twinkey. But, sitting here now, that part of it didn't make that

73

much difference. Carla concentrated on thinking about the ten girls and boys who were their counterparts today at Lincoln; they gave what she was doing a significance and meaning. She had to keep them right up in the front of her mind to get her through the day.

No one did much work. They planned their programs, got their books and assignments, and found their way from one class to another. At the end of the day, back in the homeroom, everyone looked a little weary. It had turned out that Ellen was in all of Carla's classes, and Carla wanted to show some sign of friendship to her. She had heard a little bit about Ellen and her sisters from Hattie over the years, and she wished she had some way of getting across to Ellen that she'd like to be friends with her.

"You're taking the college course too, aren't you?" Carla asked.

Ellen nodded her head. "Yes, I am." She didn't offer anything more.

"Do you know yet where you're going?" Carla persisted.

Ellen turned her dark eyes to Carla. "To state teacher's college." She threw a bright red sweater around her shoulders.

"That's a pretty color," Carla said enthusiastically. She met Ellen's eyes and she didn't know whether they were mocking her or smiling at her.

"It's old. My aunt gave it to me." Ellen turned away, and Carla suddenly realized it was a sweater she had once given away to Hattie. She thought with a pang of all the clothes she had dumped on Hattie for her nieces. Was this what Ellen held against her? What had ever made her think that a girl like Ellen would want to wear her discarded clothes! But she hadn't known Ellen then, and Hattie had always taken the clothes readily. The truth was, however, that her image of Ellen had always been entirely different from the lovely-looking girl with the strong, determined face and the tall, beautiful figure that she was. In her mind Ellen had been a little colored girl, probably with pigtails and a round, flat face, a girl who would be delighted to get some really good clothes for a change even if they were someone else's outworn things.

Carla felt sick at heart over her own ignorance and stupidity. How could she have been so dumb and so uncaring as to assume that because a girl was colored and Hattie's niece that she was merely a blob of humanity, not someone like herself with taste and feelings, a personality, a face, an individual being? Carla thought of how the millions and millions of people in the rest of the world were meaningless to her; they must think and feel and care and dream, but only the very few individuals she actually knew were the ones who took on meaning for her. It was a frightening and shattering

75

thought, and made Carla herself feel like an insignificant tadpole in a big ocean.

Carla met Twinkey and Gadge outside. "They're a great bunch of kids." Gadge was enthusiastic. "What do you think? Aren't they wonderful?"

"You talk about them as if they were some rare species." Gadge's enthusiasm made Carla feel uncomfortable. "They're kids, like us. They're all right. I don't think they like us so much."

"What do you mean?" Gadge frowned. "Why shouldn't they like us?"

"Why should they?" Twinkey demanded. "They don't know us. As far as they're concerned, we're outsiders."

"But we're doing something to help them. I'm sure they're glad about that."

"We're not doing anything so great and special," Carla said. "So we're going to a new school in our neighborhood, where we should have been going right along."

"You two make me sick." Gadge was annoyed. "Do you need a band and a parade and some flag-waving to make you get excited about something? Whether you know it or not, this is important. Really important. Just because it's the small beginning of something doesn't make it less important!"

"Yes, I know." Carla sighed. "But we've all lived in

76

separate worlds for so long, we're going to have to learn each other's language." She watched Ellen come out of school, laughing and talking with Eugene Ritchie and a group of her own. She looked very different from the cool girl who had spoken to Carla only in monosyllables. "It's going to take time, a lot of time."

Carla wished she could walk over to Ellen and say something to her, but she wouldn't have broken into that group for anything in the world. They're as separate from us as we are from them; they don't really want to mingle with us at all. How is it all going to work out? she wondered. She walked home with Gadge and Twinkey, but her thoughts were on the beautiful colored girl, Ellen.

At home Hattie was waiting for her. "Well, how did you like the new school?" Hattie asked her eagerly.

"It's O.K., it's fine." Carla wished she could be more enthusiastic for Hattie's sake. "Your niece Ellen is in my class. We sit right next to each other."

Hattie's face was beaming. "That's fine, I'm glad to hear that. I wish your mother were alive, she'd like to see you and Ellen become friends."

"I hope we do." Carla looked up and met Hattie's eyes. She felt so inadequate and ashamed before the look on Hattie's face, a look of confidence and hope. She expects too much, Carla thought fearfully, she expects much too much. I wonder what she'd think if

77

she knew her precious niece Ellen wanted me to call her Mrs. Randall!

Dan was gay when he came in. "It's a great school. We're going to have a swell football team!"

"You'd better do some studying, not just worry about football," Hattie admonished him, but there was pride in her face as she fixed him a huge peanut-butter-and-jelly sandwich.

Carla turned away and left the kitchen. She felt sad even though today had been an important step. But it was all so late. She was afraid it was too late for Ellen and herself to become friends, too late for her to get to know Hattie, really, to get behind Hattie's cheery façade. Maybe Dan would take the change better, because he was a boy and younger. Carla could hear the two of them laughing together in the kitchen. She was glad that Dan was staying in to talk with Hattie for a bit. She felt that Hattie would have liked to talk with her, but she couldn't. And so far she couldn't talk with Ellen either!

CHAPTER 6

"WHAT have you got against Carla Monroe?" Aunt Hattie was vigorously beating eggs for a cake. Ellen was sitting at the kitchen table, despondently staring ahead of her.

"I have nothing against her. Not really." Ellen knew that her aunt was staring at her, but she avoided meeting her eyes.

"You make me sick." There was impatience and worry in Aunt Hattie's voice.

"You don't know anything about it! I wish you'd leave me alone." Ellen looked up at Aunt Hattie with defiant eyes. "I'm sorry," she added with a sigh, "but you just don't understand."

"I understand more than you think I do. You're scared of Carla, that's what makes me mad. You've got nothing to be scared of or to be ashamed of. You're good-looking and you've got brains. Carla would like to be friends with you, she told me so. But she needs some encouragement."

"Well, I'm afraid she's not going to get it from me."

There were some things Ellen couldn't talk about. She didn't care about Carla and her girl friend Twinkey and her boy friend Gadge, and all the rest of them. She wasn't afraid of them, she was positive of that. She just didn't want to make friends with them or to hang around with them. Maybe because *they* wanted to be friends, she didn't want to give them the satisfaction. She remembered something her father had said a long time ago, that the trouble with most white folks is that if they have one friend who is a Negro, they go around puffed out as if they've solved the whole race question. She knew her feelings were partly mixed up with that, but she didn't want to delve into the matter too deeply. She was perfectly content to keep to her own friends and avoid the others. But she wished that Aunt Hattie would mind her own business and leave her alone! She was also tired of being reminded of her beauty and brains and that she could be *somebody*. Somebody to Aunt Hattie meant someone who was "a credit to the race," making her feel like an ornamental piece to be shown off, like the family's good china.

"One of these days I'm going to invite Carla and Dan over here, and you'll have to be nice to them."

Aunt Hattie's face was so smug and she looked so pleased with herself that Ellen had to laugh. "You think you're smart, Aunt Hattie. Go ahead, invite them, see if I care. They'll be your guests, not mine, and I won't do a thing! Maybe I won't even be home," she added slyly.

"You're a devil." Aunt Hattie poured the batter into the cake pans and gently put them into the oven. She laughed to herself at the idea of inviting Carla and Dan over to dinner. She just might do it at that.

Ellen and Aunt Hattie were still sitting in the kitchen when Mr. Randall came home. His calm face was bright with a concealed excitement. "What are you so het up about?" Aunt Hattie eyed him shrewdly.

"What makes you think I'm het up about anything?" Mr. Randall said with a grin. "I'm feeling good, is that bad?"

"You never had a poker face, George Randall, and you never were able to fool me from the day you were born. Something's got you excited."

"Maybe he has a secret," Ellen said good-naturedly.

"That's right. Maybe I've got a secret." Mr. Randall's face was all smiles as if he knew, just as well as Aunt Hattie, that he'd have a hard time keeping a secret from her.

"Well, if it's such a happy secret, you might as well make us happy too." Aunt Hattie's nose was sniffing like a fox terrier on a scent.

Mr. Randall shrugged. "It's not really a secret. And it's just a rumor. There's nothing to it, nothing at all."

"Will you stop standing there like a kid and tell us

what it's all about!" Aunt Hattie demanded, hardly able to contain her impatience.

Mr. Randall deliberately filled his pipe and lit it. "As I said, it's just a rumor." He spoke carefully, slowly. "But you know the Mayor's setting up a committee to solve the integration problem in this city." There was an amused smile on Mr. Randall's face. "He's going to get it all straightened out in Thomasville with his committee. Well, I guess it won't hurt any," he added kindly. "The talk is that Mr. Monoe's going to head it up. That's the only good thing about the committee that I've heard so far. Maybe they'll really do something if Monroe's in charge."

"That's good news. Good news." Aunt Hattie was pleased. "At least we've got them moving in this town. Something good is bound to come of it."

"I suppose," Mr. Randall said, "but I haven't gotten to my real news yet."

"Oh, Daddy, what is it?" Ellen had hoped it was something more than just another committee.

"Just hold on, I'll get there. We had a meeting of our own committee this afternoon." Mr. Randall mentioned the leading men in the Negro community, the ministers, teachers, lawyers, and businessmen. "They all think Monroe will offer me a job on his commission. They want me to take it."

"Oh, Daddy, that would be wonderful!" Ellen's eyes were shining with pride. "Wouldn't that be terrific!"

"Don't get too excited. It hasn't happened yet." But Mr. Randall could not conceal the hope and excitement in his face. His eyes were glowing the way Eugene's did when Eugene talked about being an architect. Ellen thought of her mother's words about a new hope for their Negro men, and she realized how painful it must have been for her mother too, all these years, to watch her father plod along defeated by life. Now that she herself was in love, and was going through all the nuances, the delicate complications of identifying closely with a boy, she could see more clearly the strength of her mother's love for her father. "Negro women have to love their men a little more than other women do," Nellie had also said, and Ellen was beginning to understand what she meant.

"I'll have Mr. Monroe behind me." Mr. Randall was thinking out loud. "Maybe a couple of others. I'm not thinking of just myself, it would be a good thing for the whole community. It isn't just a job for me that's important, although I don't mind admitting I would sure like to get behind a drawing board again. I was thinking of dropping around to see Mr. Monroe tonight, but maybe I won't. I'll wait for him to come to me. Yes, that'll be better."

"How do you know he will?" Ellen asked.

Mr. Randall laughed. "I know him. He'll be around."

"I've been telling Ellen she should make friends with Carla. You talk to her. That daughter of yours sometimes gets me mad." Aunt Hattie shook her head and looked with annoyance at Ellen.

"Let her pick her own friends," Mr. Randall said gently. But he turned to Ellen. "Carla's a nice girl. Jake Monroe's been good to me, and I'd be proud to have you and his daughter be friends."

Ellen didn't say anything. She knew what her father meant, although she resented his use of the word *proud*. She got up and went upstairs to her room. Although it was tiny, Ellen had a room of her own, and it was her pride and her refuge. She came here to be alone, to think, to luxuriate in her aloneness.

The funny thing was that what she had seen of Carla Monroe so far she liked. Carla often leaned over to her during class to whisper little side remarks and jokes that made Ellen laugh. Carla was as friendly as anyone could be, and Ellen felt that she was eager to make their friendship more intimate. But each time Carla seemed about to make a move, Ellen found herself withdrawing and not giving her a chance. It was an automatic reaction, like pulling one's hand away from a fire.

Maybe she was being stupid, Ellen now argued with herself. She had no reason to distrust Carla, and it was

84

wrong for her to hold the girl's white skin against her. She wanted Carla to make all the advances, to come not only halfway, but all the way, and she knew that Carla would never do that. It would take an effort from both of them to become friends.

Ellen stared at her own reflection in the glass. What did Carla see when she looked at her? Did she see just the dark skin and the heavy black hair, or did she see a human being, a girl like herself with feelings and thoughts and hopes and dreams? Ellen wasn't sure, but she decided she would give Carla a chance, she would really try to accept and return her overtures at friendship.

The senior class was electing its new president and other officers for the year. There wasn't much interest in the election; everyone took for granted that Eugene would be president, and it didn't matter too much who the others were. As was expected, Eugene was the only person put up for president, and he was elected unanimously.

Ellen was totally surprised to hear her own name nominated for vice-president and seconded by a loud chorus. While she was flattered and pleased with the nomination, she was not at all sure she wanted the office. She didn't really like to be bothered with a lot of meetings and worry, and true to her nature she was quite content to let someone else take on the leadership required.

Ellen looked around the room to see who else might be good for the job, and suddenly she had a brainstorm. She was never one for making speeches, and she stood up timidly. "I would like to nominate Carla Monroe," she spoke in a low, clear voice. "We have attached great importance to having this school even partially integrated, so I think the vice-president should be one of our new students. You all said that a girl should have the office, and Carla can contribute a lot of experience she's had over at Lincoln that we can use here. I withdraw in her favor, and I think it's great that these kids are coming to our school."

Ellen sat down, looking neither to left nor right, but she heard an enthusiastic second to the nomination. Carla was elected unanimously. After the elections were over, Ellen left the room hurriedly to go to her next class. She heard Carla call after her, but she pretended not to hear. She felt embarrassed and flustered, and she didn't want Carla to thank her, or to say anything at all. She had done the whole thing so suddenly and so quickly, she hadn't thought it through to what would happen afterward. But she was glad she had nominated Carla. It would have been stupid to have an all-Negro slate of officers, and maybe this election would help break the ice between the groups.

Eugene, a happy smile on his face, caught up with Ellen. "What's your hurry? What are you running away from?" He took her by the arm.

"I'm going down to the chem lab. I have some experiments to do."

"That was a great idea of yours, honey. Good thinking. I like that girl Carla."

"I don't know where I got the nerve. I've never done anything like that before in my life."

"See, it wasn't so hard, was it? You should speak up more often." Eugene's eyes sobered. "I guess we all have to start doing things we've never done before."

"Now stop preaching race to me. You know I'm getting tired of thinking about my race."

"Yeah, I know. But that was a good thing you did, Ellen. I'm glad you did it."

"It's nothing to get excited about," she said casually, but she felt a warm glow of pleasure at her own temerity.

When Ellen came down to the school cafeteria for lunch, Carla was waiting at the door. She smiled at Ellen. "I've been waiting for you. Will you have lunch with me?"

Ellen hesitated for a second. "Yes, of course. I'd like to."

"Let's get our trays. Oh, good, there's tuna-fish salad. I love it, I could eat it every day. Do you want some?"

"Yes, sure." Tuna fish was not Ellen's favorite dish, but she wanted to be friendly and agreeable. She hoped Carla would do the talking, because she didn't think she'd know what to say.

Carla led the way to a table over in a corner where they could be alone.

"You did a very nice thing this morning," Carla said, when they had emptied their trays and were settled at the table eating their salad.

"I thought you'd be good for the job," Ellen said.

"Thank you. But you were just guessing, you don't really know me. Ellen, what you did was more than just nominate someone to be vice-president, it was. . . ." Carla hesitated in embarrassment. She wanted to pour out her feelings to Ellen, to tell her how much she wanted to be friends, but she was afraid Ellen would rebuff her. This morning had seemed like a breakthrough, the first recognition that Ellen, too, wanted to break down the wall and to make friends.

Ellen nodded her head. "I know what you mean. I guess I've been acting kind of silly. . . . But, well, I guess you'll never understand."

Carla sighed. "I can't pretend to understand how you feel, but I can try. With all the barriers between us, I guess we can't be close friends naturally. We have

88

to work at it a little." She leaned over the table toward Ellen. "I'd love it if you'd come home from school with me this afternoon. Hattie's been bawling me out because we haven't been friendly."

Ellen laughed. "She's been after me too, telling me that it's all my fault!"

Carla laughed with her. "I guess she's been giving us both the same line. Will you come over this afternoon?"

Ellen nodded. "Sure, I'd love it, thanks a lot."

Both girls were relieved to find that Hattie had gone when they came into the Monroe kitchen. Neither one of them wanted her watchful eye overlooking their first visit together. "Want something to eat?" Carla took out peanut butter and jelly and made them both sandwiches. She gave Ellen a Coke and took one herself.

"How about me? Don't I get anything?" Dan came into the kitchen to join them. If he was surprised to see Ellen there, he didn't show it.

"Help yourself." Dan made himself a huge sandwich and sat down on the kitchen table facing the girls. "That school is really behind," he said. "They're doing math in the ninth grade that we did two years ago."

"My father's been saying that for years," Ellen said. She liked Dan; he was natural and said what he thought.

"I hope they do something about it." Dan looked

directly at Ellen. "Everybody's not going to fold up now about this school, I hope. That Board of Ed should make one of the schools a high and the other elementary. The way they have it now is cockeyed."

"I know. That's what we really want. But I don't know. . . ."

"It takes time," Carla said.

Ellen moved around restlessly. That was an expression she was beginning to be sick of hearing. It takes time, it takes time. . . .

"Do you want to come up to my room?" Carla asked. She didn't want to talk to Ellen about school and race problems. She wanted to get behind Ellen's cool, remote face, to talk to her really, but she didn't know how to get started.

Upstairs she put on a record and the girls talked a little while the music was playing. "I'm glad Eugene got elected president. He's your boy friend, isn't he?" Carla asked.

Ellen nodded. "We've been going together for almost three years. Do you have a boy friend?"

Carla sighed. "Well, yes and no. I guess you could call Gadge my boy friend, we see each other all the time. But I think I'm falling in love with someone else."

"I'll never love anyone but Eugene," Ellen said emphatically. "Never. I don't care who I meet."

"But I wasn't in love with Gadge, I never really was. I like him a lot, but this is different. This boy is older than we are, and he doesn't even know the way I feel about him. He's a law student who works in my father's office."

Ellen's eyes were sympathetic. "That must be awful, to love someone who doesn't love you back. I couldn't bear it if Eugene ever stopped loving me. I just couldn't bear it."

"But doesn't it bother you to be in love when you're so young? You can meet so many people yet."

"I don't think about anyone but Eugene. I just feel right with him, and I think he feels the same way about me. What's the sense of looking for someone else, when you've found the right person?"

"I wasn't looking for anyone. I guess Gadge just isn't the right person. But it must be wonderful to feel that you've met him. You and Eugene look just right for each other, even when you walk together."

Ellen smiled. "We are, we really are." She stood up to leave. "I've got to go home to bathe the kids and help Aunt Hattie with supper." She answered the questioning look on Carla's face. "My mother leaves for the hospital soon; she works at night."

Carla went downstairs with her to the door. "I'm glad you came over. Will you do it again soon?"

"Sure. And you can come back to my house. It was good talking to you."

When Ellen left, Carla realized with a start that for a while she had forgotten all about the color of Ellen's skin. They had talked together the way any two girls do. It gave Carla a peculiar warm feeling. It was mixed with guilt, because she had never talked to a Negro this way before, but it also gave her an extraordinary lift. She hoped that Ellen was as pleased as she.

Both Dan and Gadge went around with some of the Negro boys in school. But boys didn't have boy friends the way girls had girl friends, so it wasn't quite the same for them. Yet Carla had felt out of it and had felt that they were making something out of their new contacts at school that she was not. Now maybe things would be different for her, now she hoped that she would make her change in schools really count.

CHAPTER 7

CARLA watched the gym teacher make practice shots at the basket with a few of the Negro girls. Twinkey, sitting on the other side of the gym, was watching too. The physical-ed teacher was a problem to Twinkey and Carla. She was a squat, stern-faced young Negro woman, who bypassed Carla and Twinkey whenever she could. Now Carla screwed up her courage to speak to Ellen. "Your Miss Howard really hates us, doesn't she?"

Ellen turned around in surprise. "What do you mean? What makes you say that?"

"She never lets Twinkey or me play more than a few minutes in a game. We've both noticed that she really discriminates against us."

Ellen couldn't help but smile. "We're all a sensitive bunch around here, aren't we?" She leaned over closer to Carla. "I think she's scared of you. You aren't used to colored teachers, and they're not used to you. She probably wants you to volunteer more; she's really O.K. Go ahead and do some practicing now."

Hesitantly Carla got up, motioning to Twinkey to

join her. The two girls came over awkwardly to where the others were playing. "Can we come in?" Carla asked timidly.

Miss Howard's answer was to toss her the ball. "Go ahead, shoot."

Carla was taken by surprise, and although she was close to the basket she missed. "Sorry."

Discouraged, Carla was about to turn away, when Miss Howard called her. "Come over here. You didn't catch the ball properly for shooting it. Here, try it this way." She worked seriously and hard with Carla and Twinkey until the end of the period.

"See, I told you to try her," Ellen said, with a mixture of warmth and pride on her face.

"I'm glad I spoke to you." Carla brightened. "Ellen, let's promise always to tell each other everything. . . . I mean, anything that bothers us. To be honest with each other. It's so easy to have stupid misunderstandings."

The girls' eyes met gravely. "That sounds like a good idea. It won't always be easy. . . ."

"Of course it won't be easy. But if we want to be real friends. . . ." Carla felt flustered. She hated sticky, sentimental talk, but there were things she wanted to say. "What I mean is that you and I both know it will be hard to become really close, trusting friends. But if we talk things out instead of getting hurt and turning away, maybe it will be easier."

Ellen smiled. "I know what you mean. All we can do is try." The girls shook hands solemnly.

After that Carla felt closer to Ellen than she had ever felt to another girl, even to Twinkey. They talked about everything in the world when they were together. Of late the conversation had come around to their parents, their fathers in particular. "The minute my father walks into a room, you know it," Carla said. "I hate wishy-washy men, don't you?"

Ellen nodded her head in agreement. "That's what I love about Eugene; no one's ever going to push him around. My dad's a little beaten, I think, but still has ideals that he believes in. He's never ever going to give up, really. Say, is your father heading up that commission for the Mayor?" Ellen asked suddenly.

"I think so. He talks about it a lot. I'm sure he's dying to do it. He has to make up his mind in the next couple of days."

"I hope he does." Ellen leaned over confidentially. "I shouldn't say this, my dad would kill me if he knew, but everyone expects your father to offer my father a job on the commission." Ellen stopped to watch the effect of her words on Carla. "It would be the turning point in my dad's whole life," she added, smiling at the genuine pleasure in Carla's face. "It would make everything he's struggled for worthwhile. You've no idea what it would mean to him."

95

"I think I have," Carla said quietly. "I'm sure my father will do it. He thinks the world of Mr. Randall, and he talks about him a lot. Oh, Ellen, wouldn't it be wonderful?"

"I'll say," Ellen agreed. Her dark eyes were shining with a great intensity. "We can be proud of our fathers. I'm so glad. I'd hate to have a family that didn't do anything, that didn't believe in anything."

A few days later Mr. Monroe announced his decision to accept the Mayor's invitation to head up a commission to study the problem of integration in Thomasville. The commission was to concern itself with housing, jobs, and schools. One of its main projects would be to come up with a plan for relocating the families down by the river. The city already owned the old warehouses there, and work on razing them was to begin soon. Part of the commission's job was to get architectural plans for a housing development to be built in stages so that families could be moved from their slum houses into new ones without another move in between.

Mr. Monroe did not announce his staff, but said that he would very soon. Carla was unable to get him to talk about it. She tried every way she knew to coax out of him whom he was taking on, but he refused to talk. Finally she asked him outright if he was going to give

Mr. Randall a job. Her father was snappy and impatient. "I wish people would stop talking and worrying about my job," he said. "I have to get together a group that will work together well, and that's more important than the individual members." Carla shut up after that, but she was worried. She kept telling herself that her father would do the right thing, and she was sure that Mr. Randall would get his chance.

Hattie went around with such a beaming expression on her face that Carla wondered if she had any inside line on the subject. But when she tried to question Hattie, all she could get out of her was a wide grin and a deep chuckle. "How should I know what your father's doing? What a thing to ask me!"

Adam was just as closemouthed. Adam's self-containment, as a matter of fact, was becoming one of his most fascinating and irritating qualities to Carla. He came home to dinner fairly frequently with her father, and a few times he took Carla off to the movies. They talked about a lot of things, but he still said very little about himself, and he refused to talk about what Mr. Monroe was up to. Carla found this frustrating, but enormously provocative, and each time she saw him she was more convinced that she was deeply in love. She wasn't sure how Adam felt about her, but every once in a while she thought he must like her a lot by the way he looked at her. Her father's few teasing remarks about how Adam always wanted to come home with him, and he didn't think it was the food, also encouraged her. One of these days soon, she felt, Adam would tell her how he felt. . . . She didn't mind waiting.

Partly to give herself something else to think about, Carla decided to give a party for the kids she knew at school. The next time Carla and Ellen left school together, Carla said, "It's about time someone gave a party, and I think I'm it. What do you say?"

Ellen didn't answer, and Carla turned around to look at her. Ellen's face had closed up into its masklike inscrutability. "What's the matter?" Carla asked.

"Nothing. So you want to give a party, give it."

Carla stopped walking and stood still. "Come off it, Ellen. What's eating you? Remember, you and I promised we'd be absolutely honest with each other."

"What kind of a party do you have in mind?" Ellen asked after a few minutes.

"An ordinary party. You and Eugene, Twinkey and someone, Gadge and me, and I'd like you to ask a few friends, and I'd ask a few kids, and we'd have a party." The girls continued walking.

Ellen studied Carla's face. "You're not very bright," she said. "There have never been any mixed parties for teen-agers in Thomasville. What makes you think people will come?"

"My friends will come. How about yours?" Carla met Ellen's gaze serenely.

"I guess they'll come." Her face broke into a smile. "Do them good to travel in high society for a change."

"We're not high society," Carla said indignantly. "Listen, Ellen, if there haven't been any mixed parties it's high time they were started. We couldn't have them before when everyone went to different schools, but now we're all friends, aren't we?"

"Some of us are," Ellen said soberly. "You know, we've been going along as if everything's been solved. It's far from it. My folks are getting impatient about this silly token gesture with the school."

"What are they going to do about it?"

"They're planning a demonstration in front of the school-board building. I think they're also going to send a delegation to meet with your father when he gets his commission set up. He's supposed to be looking into the school situation too."

"I'm sure my father will do everything he can. If your father is on the commission too, something will certainly happen. You wait and see."

"I'm waiting all right," Ellen said.

"But none of this is any reason we can't have a party, is it? I mean your friends don't hold it against us, do they?" Carla asked frankly.

"They're all mixed up. Some of them criticize us.

They say we're too friendly with the whites, but I think they're stupid. If they want integration, it's got to work two ways."

"Will you ask them to a party?" Carla came to the point.

"Sure, I'll ask them. How many, and when?"

"What about Saturday night? This is only Tuesday, that'll give us plenty of time. Let's see . . . we're four, and there's Twinkey and a date. Why don't you ask two more couples, and I'll ask one more. That'll make twelve, sounds like just the right size for a party, don't you think?"

"Sounds fine. I'd like to ask my friend Minde. You haven't met her, because she graduated last year. Is that all right?"

"Sure, why not? Anyone you want. What about that pretty little girl I see you with sometimes? Helen's her name, isn't it?"

Ellen shook her head. "She won't come. She's very shy, and she hates white folks."

Carla frowned. "That's too bad. Maybe if she gave us a chance and tried to know us, she'd change her mind."

"I don't think so. Her father's in jail for stabbing someone, and her family thinks he was framed by a white cop. She wouldn't come to any party at your house."

"But that's not fair," Carla blurted out. "It's exactly the same thing that you accuse the white people of doing, lumping everyone together."

"I know, but you might feel the same way if you had to put up with what she does."

"I suppose so, but it wouldn't be very smart of me. Who else are you going to invite, Ellen?"

"I don't know. I was thinking of Jimmy Oakes, the minister's son, and the girl he goes with, Annabelle. Jimmy would come."

"Sure, his father would make him." Carla laughed. "This whole thing is ridiculous."

"Of course it is. But never mind, we'll have a wonderful party anyway. I've learned a lot just knowing you, Carla. We all used to tease Aunt Hattie about her white family, but now I know why she's so fond of you."

"Well, I'm glad somebody likes us," Carla said.

"I value your friendship a lot," Ellen said gravely. "All the preaching about the races getting together means something good to me now, instead of something I almost resented before."

"I'm glad," Carla said simply. "And whatever you've learned, you can double it for me."

Saturday afternoon Twinkey came over to help Carla get ready for the party. Carla wanted it to be the best party she had ever given. She gave great thought to the preparations. "I want it to be kind of elegant, without being too fancy," she said to Twinkey.

"What are you going to give them to eat tonight?" Twinkey asked.

"Let's have something more than just sandwiches and Cokes. I think I'll make a big pot of spaghetti and meatballs. Everyone likes that. What do you think?"

"That's a good idea. It's not fancy, but it shows a little care. Besides it's good to eat." Twinkey thought of something else. "How will we break the ice when the kids get here? I hate it when everyone sits around waiting for someone else to make a move."

"I know. What can we do?"

"Maybe we can play some crazy game to get things going. Then afterward everyone will dance, and it'll be all right. It's the beginning that's important."

Carla looked thoughtful. "We could play charades. Divide into two teams. What do you think?"

"Why don't we wait and see how it goes," Twinkey suggested. "One of us can always suggest charades if we need to."

"That's a good idea," Carla agreed.

The two girls went out marketing to buy food and soda for the evening, and then together made the meatballs and spaghetti sauce. When Twinkey went home, Carla got supper ready for her father, Dan, and herself.

"You're not getting much of a supper tonight," she

announced to them. "There will be spaghetti and meat-balls to eat later."

"You're going all out for this party," Dan remarked.

"I certainly am," Carla told him. "I want it to be the best party ever."

"What's new downtown?" Dan asked his father at the supper table. Mr. Monroe was more preoccupied than ever since he had started his new job.

"A delegation came to see me today. The colored people aren't happy about the school situation. They say the Board of Education is ducking the issue. But what can I do? Everyone knows how I feel about it, but I'm not on the Board of Ed."

"People look up to you," Carla said admiringly. "They know that you're a fighter, and you'll stand up for what's right."

"But I'm not a miracle man." Mr. Monroe looked worried. "You can't go too far ahead of the people. Sometimes you do more harm than good if you don't gauge the tempo of the people correctly. No one can expect miracles." He repeated the word wistfully, as if he were hoping against hope to witness a miracle himself.

"Are you staying home tonight?" Carla asked him.

Her father gave her a puzzled look. "You're having a party, aren't you? Of course I'm staying home. But I won't be in your way," he added hastily.

"I'm not worried about that. I want you to meet the kids when they get here anyway. They've all heard about you, and I think they'd like to meet you." Carla looked at her father proudly.

Mr. Monroe's smile lit up his face. "I'll be glad to meet them, and I'm glad you're giving this party, Carla. It's a good thing."

"What about you, Dan? Will you be around?"

"I'll stay around for a while if you want. Then I'm going to the movies."

"That's fine."

Carla dressed for her party carefully. She wished that Adam were going to be there, but she felt she couldn't ask him with a high-school crowd. He'd think they were all too childish, and besides she couldn't do that to Gadge. It was terrible to be in love with someone whom she only saw now and then, but she didn't care. Loving Adam was a private secret that she could think about when a lot of other things were going on or whenever she was alone: walking down a street, putting rollers in her hair, or lying in bed at night. Right now it didn't even matter that she wasn't sure if he loved her back, or even knew that she loved him, although she realized that a time would come when she would need to express her love and to know how he felt about her. But she

104

was not quite ready for that yet and was content to get used to her own feelings for the time being.

A few minutes past eight Carla's guests began to arrive. Gadge and Twinkey, and Twinkey's date, Hank Frisbie, a senior who went to Lincoln, came first. Ellen and Eugene and their friends arrived soon after. It was one of those wonderful parties that click right from the start. Ellen was the one who made it work. She didn't give people a chance to stand around wondering whether the Negro boys were going to ask the white girls to dance or whether everyone was going to stick to his own date. She immediately suggested a "stop-the-music" dance, where each time the record stopped everyone had to switch partners with the couple nearest him. It was noisy and gay. "Here. . . ." Ellen pushed Eugene at Carla and grabbed hold of Gadge. "Show me those tricky steps of yours," she said gaily. Carla had never seen this Ellen, gliding about the room with her face shining, and looking as if she wanted to hug everyone, making them all seem brighter and more attractive than usual.

"I am so happy to be here," she said to Carla. "You make everyone feel so much at home. It's a lovely party." Her eyes shot across the room to Eugene, sitting on a sofa talking intently with Mr. Monroe. The two had been talking together for a long time. Whenever Carla flitted by them she caught snatches of their conversation and knew they were on Eugene's favorite topics—architecture and contemporary housing. Second to law, they were also favorite topics of her father. They were talking about Eero Saarinen and Frank Lloyd Wright, population increases, city planning, urban development. . . . Carla was sure that by this time the two of them had replanned all of Thomasville and built houses for everyone.

When Mr. Monroe finally got up and said he'd better let Eugene go back to the party, he came over to Carla. "That's a brilliant young man," her father said. "He's read everything and he knows what he's talking about."

"He's dying to be an architect. But what chance has he got? Have you ever heard of a Negro architect?"

"There are going to be a lot of things in his and your lifetime that I've never heard of," Mr. Monroe said confidently. "That boy will get there, you'll see."

"He'll have to get through college and graduate school first, and that takes money that he hasn't got."

"If a kid really wants to go to college, he'll find a way. He can work too."

"Sure, I know. But it's not all that easy, and you've got to be pretty sure you'll get a job when you graduate. Eugene's a little cynical about that. He says, look at Mr. Randall with all his education. But I told him to wait and see. Mr. Randall will get his chance." She gave her father a meaningful look.

"George's not so bad off with his teaching job," her father said and turned away. Soon after that he said good-night and went upstairs to bed.

A little before midnight someone turned on the radio instead of the record player for dance music. At midnight the news came on and a small group gathered around listening to it. After the weather report a local newspaperman, who ran a column in the Thomasville daily, came on with his Saturday-night attempt to imitate Drew Pearson with his own combination of the latest scandals and mud slinging. Someone was just about to turn him off, when Carla heard her father's name mentioned. "Jake Monroe, a prominent lawyer, has put his head in the noose the first week of his new job heading up the Mayor's commission on integration. . . ." There was total silence in the room as everyone stopped to listen. "He has come up with a lily-white pure executive staff. The only Negroes on his payroll will be a forty-dollar-a-week file clerk and a sixty-dollar-a-week secretary. I predict that his commission will fall flat on its face and will cause a wider rift in the Negro and white population of Thomasville; I predict that the Negro community, led by an old friend of Jake's, a very disappointed man tonight, will boycott the commission and everything they propose to do. How come Jake Monroe is such a big integrationist, when he can't find a job for an old friend with a college degree? Maybe Monroe has his own fish to fry. . . . The current divorce between. . . ." Someone switched off the radio.

There was a dead silence in the room. Gadge was the first one to speak. "A rat like that shouldn't be given air time. He doesn't give a hang about anything or anyone. He's just out to smash everyone."

Carla looked at Ellen's face. The laughter had gone out of it; it was cold and stern now. "It's not true, Ellen," Carla said. "I don't believe a word of it. It's not true."

"He can't make up a story like that." Ellen spoke in a tired voice. "Even he couldn't get away with that. I'm sorry to break up your party, but I think I'd like to go home." She looked at Eugene. He watched her uncertainly, but didn't make a move to do anything.

"I just don't believe it," Carla repeated emphatically. "I'm going upstairs to ask my father. He thinks the world of Mr. Randall, Ellen. I know he wants him on the staff."

Carla ran up the steps to her father's room. The door was closed and the room dark. Carla knocked on the door gently, there was no answer. She opened it and could hear her father's even breathing. She hated to wake him up, but this was too important. She had to hear the truth directly from him.

"Daddy, Daddy. . . ." Her father sat up in bed, and Carla switched on a small bedside light.

Mr. Monroe rubbed his eyes against the light. "What's the matter? What's happened?" He was suddenly wide awake.

"We had the radio on downstairs. That stinker Cliff Carter, that phony newspaperman, said that you didn't give Mr. Randall a job. He said you had a lily-white executive staff and that the commission is going to fall flat on its face. It's not true, is it Daddy?" Carla was breathless, her eyes eagerly scanning her father's face.

Mr. Monroe stretched out his arm and took a cigarette from the pack beside his bed. He lit it thoughtfully. "That son of a gun," he murmured under his breath. "I wish he hadn't done this."

"But it's not true? You can sue him for saying things like that, can't you?" Carla's face was white and tense.

"Carla, I was going to tell you in my own time. You and Dan. I can't take Mr. Randall on my staff. I wanted to very much, you've no idea how much, but in all fairness to the whole project it couldn't be done. The worst reactionaries, men like Cliff Carter, those who don't care at all about the Negro people, are going to make a thing of this, but that's the sad part about taking on a public job. People jump to conclusions without knowing the facts, and distort the truth for their own purposes. The truth the matter is that Mr.

Randall is not really qualified for the job he wanted. He has never had a day's practical experience, and he got his college degree many years ago in a third-rate school. It is very tough on him, but this is exactly the condition we are working to cure. I'm afraid it's too late for the George Randalls. . . . Let's hope that the next generation, like that Ritchie boy downstairs, will benefit. We've got to make it work for them."

Carla sat silently while her father was speaking, her eyes roaming around the room and coming back to his face. "But you're talking about formalities, degrees and experience," Carla said. "You know Mr. Randall as a man. You know he could probably do it, and only someone like you could give him a chance."

"If it were my own business, I'd give him a chance in a minute. But I'm spending public money, tax money, and I can't gamble with it. The risk is too great. I have to hire the best brains in the business for this job, people with experience. Everything I do will be under close scrutiny; my plans and budget have to pass a Board of Estimate. If I hired George Randall, that rat Cliff Carter would be the first to attack me for hiring someone with no experience. Don't you understand? Carter and his crowd want to wreck this thing no matter what I do. They don't care about Mr. Randall. Whatever I do will be wrong for them, because they don't want change and progress; they don't want good public housing for anyone; all they care about is keeping taxes down."

Carla sat quietly with her shoulders slumped. It was hard to believe that people could be so evil. She didn't want to look at her father's face. She felt as if she were swimming in a sea way beyond her depth, she felt panicky and confused, wishing she could reach out and grab hold of something solid. In all her life she had never doubted her father. She had always believed completely in his judgment, in his knowledge of facts, in his principles. As far as she was concerned he could do no wrong, but now for the first time the vaguest hint of a doubt crossed her mind. How could she know that he was absolutely right in what he was doing? What if he were wrong, if he were mistaken and had misjudged Mr. Randall's ability? What if he were wrecking Mr. Randall's life unnecessarily?

"How do you know you're right?" she asked her father finally. "How do you know that if you had taken Mr. Randall on, it wouldn't work out all right?"

Mr. Monroe took a long time answering. "I don't know," he said, inhaling deeply on his second cigarette. "I don't know absolutely and for sure. There is no way of knowing. But after I considered the matter every which way, and don't think I haven't been thinking about it for a long while, I decided this was the right thing for the city of Thomasville as a whole and for the Negro people in it. That's all I can say." He leaned toward Carla with a soft, almost wistful plea in his eyes that she had never seen in them before. "I have to do what I think best. I wish you could trust me, trust my judgment. I need your faith in me."

Carla pulled her eyes away from his. "I have to think about it, Daddy. You told me once no one should have blind faith, that faith only has meaning if we understand exactly what it is we believe in. You said that blind faith is ignorant, that a free people must know what they believe in and have faith in themselves."

"Yes, I said all that." Her father sighed. "But sometimes love requires faith, a different kind of faith. If you love someone, you have to have faith in him sometimes even if you don't understand what he is doing. Don't come to any hasty conclusions, Carla."

"I'll try not to. But I wish. . . . I wish it were the other way around. I wish you had given Mr. Randall the job. Then I think we could fight like anything to keep the Cliff Carters quiet. But this way. . . . I don't know, I just don't like it."

"You're very shrewd, Daughter. This way they have me on the defensive, I know that. But I didn't base my decision on what was easiest for me. I'm just doing what I think best."

"I know," Carla said, but she wasn't sure she believed it wholeheartedly. Again a wave of doubt left her feeling miserable. She stood up. "I'd better go back to my party. I don't know what to say to Ellen . . . . She feels awful."

"I hope her father will understand. I'll try to talk to him tomorrow myself." Mr. Monroe held out his hand. "Have a little faith in me, Carla." Carla took his hand in hers. She wanted to bend over and hug her father, but she felt a strain between them. They never were demonstrative, and now the gesture would be false and sentimental. Carla's heart was heavy as she left her father's room and went back downstairs to her guests.

CHAPTER 8

HURT and bewildered, Carla looked around the almost empty room. Only Gadge was there, with Twinkey, the Frisbie boy, and Dan. "Where is everybody?" She looked at Gadge accusingly, as if he should have made everyone stay.

"They left," Gadge told her quietly. "It's just as well, they were about ready to go home anyway."

"I don't think so," Carla said. She slumped down into a chair. "Nobody ate anything," she said irrelevantly, glancing at the big bowl of spaghetti and meatballs and the half-eaten remains on the paper plates. "The party was really building up, and now it's all over. It's nothing."

"What did Dad say?" Dan asked. Gadge had told him what happened, and he was eager to hear Carla's report.

"It's true." Carla spoke in a flat voice. "He didn't hire Mr. Randall. He has his own reasons, he'll have to explain them to you."

"I'm sure he has very good reasons," Dan said.

114

Carla looked at him. "Everyone has good reasons for doing what they want to do."

"That's not fair. That's a lousy thing to say," Dan cried indignantly. "Don't you think Dad would have given Mr. Randall a chance if he could? Why wouldn't he?"

"I don't know." Carla was close to tears. "I don't know," she repeated, "but you don't know what the job means to Mr. Randall, to that whole family. They were all counting on it!"

"Maybe Mr. Randall won't mind as much as you think he will," Gadge said consolingly. "He'll probably understand why your father did what he's doing."

"I doubt it," Carla said curtly, "I doubt it very much. If you don't mind, I think I'm going out for a walk," she announced.

The others exchanged startled glances. "You can't go walking by yourself at this hour of the night—the morning, I should say. It's almost one o'clock. Don't be silly, Carla." Twinkey came over to Carla. "We're leaving now, and you go to bed." She kissed Carla good-bye. "It really was a lovely party. Everyone had a good time."

"You and Hank go along," Gadge said. "I'm going to stay a few minutes."

Dan took the hint, said good-night, and went upstairs to bed, leaving Carla and Gadge alone. Gadge pulled Carla down on the sofa beside him. "You don't have to be mad at me," he said with a grin.

"I feel mad at everyone right now," Carla said, but she attempted a smile. "I'm not really mad, it's just —I feel awful, Gadge."

"What did your father say?"

Carla told him Mr. Monroe's explanation. "The trouble is," she added, "there's no way of knowing whether he's right or wrong."

"There never is," Gadge said. "I've thought of that often. If you make a choice about something, you never know how it would have turned out if you chose the other way. But I think you're taking it too hard."

Carla looked up at him. "I'm taking it hard because it's important. I've been worshiping my father blindly. I don't know any girl who feels about her father the way I do. I . . . ." Carla couldn't hold back her tears any longer. "I feel betrayed," she sobbed against the rough fabric of Gadge's jacket. "My father's the one who got me started on this whole race business in the first place, and now I feel as if he's a hypocrite like everyone else." Carla tried to stop her sobs. "There, I've said it. I didn't want to say it out loud, but that's what I've been thinking. And it makes me sick." She sat up and dried her eyes with Gadge's handkerchief; then she stood up. "I don't care what anyone says, I'm going for a walk. I couldn't go to sleep now anyway."

"Then I'll go with you." Gadge stood up too. "Whether you like it or not."

"I don't care," Carla said crossly.

It was a cold, bright night, so bright that Carla thought it ridiculous for anyone to have to walk with her, but she didn't say so. Actually she didn't mind having Gadge beside her while she sorted out the confused thoughts chasing through her mind. Gadge was understanding, he wouldn't talk if he knew she wanted to be quiet, and he would listen if she wanted to talk. Carla realized with a pang how much she had been counting on her father's being the key person in the delicate interracial negotiations, how she had visualized him as the hero of the day. She wanted so badly to prove to Ellen that there were white people who could be trusted, who really practiced what they preached, and now she felt they were sliding backward. Ellen would never trust anyone again.

Suddenly she thought of Adam. What did Adam think of this? Did he agree with her father or did he think Mr. Monroe was making a mistake? Carla wished she could talk to Adam right now, and then she realized with dismay that the next day was Sunday. She couldn't reach him until Monday, as she felt timid about calling him at his apartment. "What do you think?" she asked, turning to Gadge. "I hate that Cliff Carter, but he does have a point that Mr. Randall should get a job, don't you think?"

"I wouldn't agree with anything Carter had to say! I don't know a thing about the whole situation, so I can't judge whether your father's right or wrong. But don't get brainwashed by a fellow like Carter. If you fall for his line, think of how many other people will. That's what bothers me."

"My father shouldn't have given Carter anything to hang on to."

"Carter will try to kill this commission no matter what," Gadge said.

"My father said that too. I guess I can't think anymore. I wish I knew what to do about Ellen. If only she hadn't left that way, maybe I wouldn't feel so awful. Everything's ruined."

"You ought to call up Ellen tomorrow, try to see her. You'll be able to talk to her, I'm sure."

"I hope so. Let's walk past her house now. If the lights are on and she's up, maybe we can both talk to her. What do you think?"

"It's awfully late. Well, we can walk by, anyway."

Carla realized she had never ventured into the Negro neighborhood after dark. She didn't remember anyone's specifically telling her not to, yet she and her friends took it for granted. Carla held Gadge's arm as they walked down the quiet, darkened streets, the only sound the *rap-rap* of Carla's heels on the pavement. "Do you think it's all right?" Carla whispered.

Gadge laughed. "Who's prejudiced now? I don't think this neighborhood is different from ours. Families live here too."

Carla jumped as a car came zooming around the corner, pulled up beside them, and the driver turned a flashlight on their faces. "Oh, what are you doing here?" The round-faced policeman's voice was surprised. "You shouldn't be wandering around here at this hour."

"We're just going for a walk," Gadge said with dignity. "We're not doing anything wrong."

"I'd hate to pick you up with a knife sticking in your back. Go on home or walk someplace else."

Gadge opened his mouth to speak, but Carla hushed him up. "Come on, Gadge. We'll go home, Officer, don't worry about us." She pulled Gadge around. "I'll see Ellen tomorrow."

The police car drove away, and Gadge exploded. "Boy, does that make me mad! A knife sticking in my back! Where does he get that stuff from? If we were walking anyplace else, he wouldn't give a hoot. Because it's a Negro neighborhood, he's sure it's not safe."

"Maybe it isn't safe. Maybe they've had trouble there," Carla suggested.

Gadge's face was screwed up in disgust. "It's a family

neighborhood, the block where the Randalls live. We were as safe there as anyplace else. If he told me the whole city wasn't safe, maybe I'd believe him. But not just there!"

At Carla's house Gadge bent over to kiss her good-night. Her response was perfunctory. Gadge was a nice boy, she really did like him, but her heart was yearning for Adam.

Carla did not get a good night's rest. It took her hours and hours to fall asleep, and when she did sleep she had unpleasant, nightmarish dreams about getting stabbed. Adam was trying to rescue her, but every time he almost reached her, she receded farther away from him. When she woke up on Sunday morning she was exhausted, but there were two things that she wanted to do: first was to see Ellen, and second was to get up her courage to call Adam, hoping she could see him.

Mr. Monroe and Dan had both had breakfast when Carla came downstairs. Dan had gone out and Mr. Monroe was reading the newspapers. Carla greeted her father uneasily. For the first time in her life she felt embarrassed with him, as if now she were betraying him instead of the other way around. She felt guilty and ashamed of her unhappy thoughts about him.

"What's Carter got to say today?" she asked.

"I don't know. I never read his rubbish."

"But it's probably all about you. Don't you care?"

"Why should I care? Everyone knows he's a trouble-maker." Mr. Monroe went back to his paper.

"A lot of people read him and believe every word he says. I'm going to read him anyway."

Carla riffled through the paper until she came to Carter's column. She let out a groan of agony as she read it. "It's all about you, even worse than what he said last night." She handed her father the paper. "Read it yourself."

Mr. Monroe read through the column with an amused smile on his face. "I told you, it's all lies and rubbish."

"Can't you sue him?"

"I wouldn't bother. What he's saying is not really libelous; he's too crafty for that. I'm not worried."

Carla's eyes flashed. "But I am. I don't understand how you can be so nonchalant about this!"

Mr. Monroe put down his paper. "I am far from non-chalant, believe me. I am very much concerned about the attacks the commission is going to have to face, and the people who want it to be a failure. That is precisely why I did not offer George Randall a job. But I'm not going to get myself in a stew about Cliff Carter. He's not worth it."

Carla again felt her uneasy wave of doubt. Her father's mouth was set in a grim, determined line, his eyes were cool and faraway. Did he really know what he was doing? If there were only someone she could go to who could tell her the truth and the facts. Did she have to revise all her thinking about her father? Carla could remember times when her mother's eyes had been sad and red-rimmed from weeping, times when strange voices, loud and angry, had called up for her father on the telephone, but it had always been the other people who were wrong, never her father.

Carla sighed heavily, and poured a cup of black coffee for herself. Was her father really a dedicated, lone voice for justice, or was he an arrogant man who wanted his own way? She felt frightened and alone, as if she were suddenly losing something safe and secure, as if everything she knew and valued were trembling beneath her. This must be the way people feel in an earthquake, she thought, afraid of her own fears.

She wasn't hungry, and she was impatient to get out, so she drank down her coffee quickly, rinsed out her cup, and went off to Ellen's.

The street had its Sunday quietness, and, walking down the row of two-family houses to the Randalls', Carla thought how ridiculous it had been to be afraid last night. People with flowerpots on the windowsills and lace curtains at the windows couldn't be very dangerous. As she approached the Randall house, she became nervous about the reception she would get. She had never been there before, and she hoped she wasn't being rude dropping in on them this way. She had purposely not telephoned Ellen, because she preferred to talk to her face to face. Timidly Carla knocked on the door, and was relieved to hear Hattie's voice call out to come in.

Everyone was apparently in the back of the house in the kitchen. Carla walked through a simple hallway to the kitchen where the whole family seemed to be gathered. She felt her face flush with embarrassment as everyone turned in her direction. It was just the Randall family, but the kitchen seemed stuffed with people and children. Mr. Randall stood up to greet her, and Ellen introduced her to her mother and to the little girls, but Carla felt an uneasy tension in the room, and she wished she hadn't come.

"I wanted to talk to you," Carla finally managed to say in a low voice to Ellen. "Could you come out for a few minutes?"

Ellen's face was cool and inscrutable, the way she used to look when Carla first knew her. "There's nothing to talk about. We were stupid; we should have known better."

"You mustn't say that, Ellen. There's another side to it. I wish you'd talk about it with me."

"Talking's never going to get us anywhere. I don't hold it against you personally, Carla, but I see things

123

differently now." She glanced over toward her father. "I see things the way my father has been seeing them for a long time. My father says he let himself get fooled for a little while, but he's come back to his senses. I don't want to talk about anything."

Carla's heart sank. The dark faces in the room were polite but impassive; even Hattie's friendly, round face looked different to her. "I'm sorry, Ellen. I'm very sorry. I guess I'd better go."

She called out good-bye hurriedly and left the house. Outside, the whole street, the children playing on the sidewalk, the dark-skinned men and women talking on the corner, now seemed hostile to her. Feeling panic, she started to run, and then forced herself to slow down her steps and to walk home with dignity.

She felt tired and defeated, as if something precious and wonderful had been within her grasp and now had been taken away. Not wanting to see her father or to talk to him, she slipped quietly up to her room. She didn't have the nerve or the energy to try to call Adam. She felt too deflated and sick at heart to do anything but to nurse her grief and her sense of loss.

CHAPTER 9

THERE was a dead silence in the Randall kitchen, broken only by the kettle coming to a boil on the stove, after Carla had left. "Want some coffee, Ellen?" Aunt Hattie asked.

"No, no thank you."

Mr. Randall glanced up at his daughter's stony face. "Don't get yourself all worked up," he said. "I never really expected to get out of teaching addition and subtraction."

Ellen didn't answer. She knew her father's remark wasn't true. In the past several weeks she had seen a light in his eyes she had never seen there before, and now his defeat was worse than it ever had been. Before any thought of a new job, he had carried a wry, amused look on his face, a look saying that this world was cock-eyed, but that he could take it. Now there was a new look of dejection, defeat, and bitterness around his mouth. And her mother too. Mrs. Randall seemed to have faded, to have withdrawn farther back into her quiet self. The only life in her face was the pain in her eyes when she looked at her husband.

"I don't understand Mr. Monroe. I just don't understand what's got into him," Aunt Hattie mumbled.

"Nothing's got into him that doesn't get into any white man's gullet when it comes to a showdown. He's scared stiff to stick his neck out, if there's a chance in the world his head will be chopped off. Jake Monroe's an ambitious man. He's got to protect himself." Mr. Randall poured his third cup of coffee.

"What are you going to do about it?" Ellen demanded of her father.

Her mother looked alarmed and came over to her husband's side. "We're no worse off than we were before. You shouldn't have pinned so much hope on it, that's the trouble."

"Why shouldn't he have hoped?" Ellen's eyes were defiant. "He had a right to hope. The trouble is we count too much on *their* doing things for us, giving out favors. We've got to do things for ourselves."

Aunt Hattie looked at her grandniece admiringly. "Well, you've certainly changed your tune. I thought by now you were in so thick with those white kids, you'd forgotten what color you are."

"You're the one who wanted me to make friends with them!" Ellen retorted sharply. "If you remember,

I'm the one who didn't want to have anything to do with them."

"I know," Aunt Hattie admitted unhappily, sighing deeply. "I know. I guess I'm the one who's the fool, thinking everyone could be nice and cozy together." She had a sad, bewildered expression on her good face, as if she didn't know what she thought or believed in.

"But Daddy, you can't just sit back and let this happen without doing something. Can't we put up a fight to get you on the commission?" Ellen was insisting.

"I don't know that it's fair to ask people to make a rumpus about one man's job. There are so many other things to worry about, things that our people need more than a job for me."

"But it isn't just your job," Ellen said eagerly. "It's the whole commission, what it stands for. If it starts out this way, what can it accomplish?"

"Well, we'll see," her father said reluctantly. "I'll talk to some of the men about it and find out what they think."

Ellen felt frustrated and impatient. It was true, she had changed practically overnight. She was angry with herself for having befriended Carla. Ellen felt she had been right in the first place not to have trusted the white people, to have wanted to steer clear of them. Now she was angry. Angry with herself for having been weak and foolish enough to think Carla could have been her friend, and angry with her father for his own resigned acceptance of the situation. She put on her coat and went outside to find Eugene. She didn't have far to go. Halfway down the block she met him on his way to her house. Eugene looked excited.

"What's up?" Ellen asked.

"Plenty. People around here are pretty sore about your father's not getting on that commission."

"What are they going to do?" Ellen asked.

"They want to have a meeting tonight. I think they want to go down and picket the Mayor's office and Mr. Monroe's office too."

Ellen sighed. "I don't know as they'll get my father to go along with them." She put her arm through Eugene's, as always finding relief just being with him. "Let's go for a walk now," she suggested.

A few blocks from their houses, the neighborhood took a decided turn for the worse. Wet marshland ran down to the river, and most of the houses were built on rickety stilts, their front steps leading to board planks set on muddy paths. The houses were forlorn-looking, bare of any lawn or trees, many windows stuffed with cardboard, their gaping doorways filled with thin children of all ages. "You don't want to walk down here." Eugene turned to go back.

"Yes, I do. Why shouldn't we walk down here?" Ellen's eyes were angry. "Isn't this where we belong?"

"No, we don't belong down here," Eugene said gently. "Nobody belongs down here. Chickens have better houses than these. Don't get bitter, Ellen. You know what this section looks like, and it's stupid to walk here."

"Well, I feel stupid!" Ellen's eyes had tears in them. "How can these people bear to live this way? And we've all accepted it for so many years. I'm just waking up, I'm just beginning to get really angry. I've been living in such a closed, blind, safe little world, thinking if I leave the white folks alone, they won't bother me. But I see how stupid that is, and I can hardly bear it, Eugene!" Ellen had stopped walking. She stood looking at the flimsy houses and the Negro children, her young face stamped with tragedy.

"It's good to get angry," Eugene said, "but I feel full of hope. I'm glad we're waking up."

Ellen put her arm through Eugene's again. "When I look at you I feel full of hope." Her eyes were proud and affectionate. "I feel we can do anything."

They walked back in silence, keeping in step with each other's long, easy stride. There was an impromptu meeting in the Randall kitchen when they returned. The minister had come there directly from church, together with some of the leading men and women of the community.

They were proposing plans for the civil rights

organization and other interested groups to demonstrate around City Hall and to throw a picket line around Mr. Monroe's office. "I hate to make Monroe the butt of this," Mr. Randall said in a worried voice. "It doesn't seem right. He's been a good friend to us."

"Sure, when he hasn't had to stick his neck out," a dark, stern-faced man said. "Monroe's made himself the butt of this, not us."

Mr. Randall still looked worried. "Maybe he thinks he's doing the right thing. We don't know."

"We know it's not right, that's what counts," someone else said.

Ellen felt pain at her father's tired, defensive air. She wanted him to be angry, to stand up and fight, she wanted his voice to be the strongest of anyone's there. She couldn't bear to see him hedging and uncertain, still defending his white friend Jake Monroe.

"But you don't understand." Mr. Randall's voice was stronger. "It was unrealistic of me, of any of us, to expect Monroe to give me a job on his staff. I've been thinking hard about this. I have had no professional experience, and I haven't used my training for twenty-five years. Everything is different now from when I studied. It was just a pipe dream to think I could get a job after all these years. I agree he should not have a lily-white professional staff, but he'd probably have to go out of town to find a qualified Negro. Maybe Monroe didn't want to do that."

"I don't care if he had to go to Howard University, to Tuskegee, Harvard, or Yale." The stern-faced man was adamant.

"I'm not so sure about that," Mr. Randall said reasonably. "You know how this town is about bringing in outsiders for good jobs. It wouldn't sit right. I'll go along with your insisting that a Negro be on the professional staff, but not if you insist that I be hired for the job. That wouldn't be right."

Mr. Randall spoke quietly, but Ellen knew that he would stubbornly defend his position. She felt pride in his quiet dignity and steadfastness in his own principles of what he considered right. He had a clear, unselfish view of the whole picture, while she had been looking for some flamboyant action, and she was ashamed of her impatience with him. Her whole body was flooded with a feeling of warmth for her father and with a happy glow that she was his daughter.

Ellen listened to the discussion and plans quietly, an idea forming in her head. Finally she got up the courage to speak. The discussion had gone on from the particular problem of the commission's staff to the more general needs of the community in the way of housing, integrated schools, and jobs for Negroes. "I think we should call all the kids out of school for the demonstration and the picket line," Ellen said. "This token business with the high school is silly. Nothing's really happened. I think we should call everyone out of school again."

Aunt Hattie looked at her grandniece in amazement. "Well, wonders will never cease! You're the girl who didn't want to boycott the school last September! Or are you a different girl?"

Ellen smiled. "I guess I am different. Aren't you glad?"

Aunt Hattie eyed her shrewdly. "I'm glad that you're learning we have to fight every inch of the way, that no one's giving us anything."

"Well, what about calling the kids out of school?" Ellen repeated. "Do you think it's a good idea?" She looked at Eugene, who had been quiet during the whole discussion.

Eugene nodded his head. "I think it's a great idea. You couldn't keep the young people out of this if you tried. They're in it and they're committed."

Everyone agreed it was a good idea, and it was suggested that Eugene and Ellen take it up with their student body and have someone represent the school at the formal organization meeting.

Ellen and Eugene went off by themselves to make their own plans for the school. Ellen felt tremendously excited to be a vital part of the demonstration, to know that she could play her own role in it, to have established this wonderfully warm rapport with her family, and with the excitement came a great sense of release and of calm.

Abruptly a new thought struck Eugene. "I wonder what Carla's going to do."

"That's her problem," Ellen said somewhat sharply. "I don't care what she does. I can't worry about her."

"It worries me," Eugene said soberly. "That picket line, and the demonstration should be integrated. But Carla may not want to picket her own father's office, and she can get all the white kids to go along with her."

"Let them go," Ellen said. "We don't need them."

"But this is a fight for the whites as well as the blacks."

"I'm not keeping them out. If they want to, they'll come along. If they don't, there's little we can do about it."

"I suppose so," Eugene said uncertainly. But he had a worried little frown between his eyes as he left for home.

CHAPTER 10

CARLA never thought of Adam's calling her today. Her thoughts were pre-occupied with how she might reach him, and her fantasies took her walking past his house just at the moment when he was coming out, or had her meeting him in a shop or on a bus. She retreated to her room filled with despair over her encounter with Ellen, thinking about Adam, and feeling miserable about her father. All the doubts about her father made her feel totally alone, as if she had discovered some hideous private secret that she must carry about with her for the rest of her life.

When the telephone rang, she almost didn't answer it. She thought it was probably Twinkey or Gadge, and she didn't feel like talking to either of them. When she recognized Adam's voice, she was dumfounded, convinced there must be mental telepathy between them, because she had been thinking about him so hard. Perhaps this was a sign of real love when two people thought about each other at exactly the same time. Adam did not talk long on the telephone. He said he wanted very much to see her, and could she have dinner with him.

In a couple of seconds the conversation was over, and Carla put the receiver back on its hook unbelievingly. A telephone's ring, and the whole world became different. All the worry didn't disappear. It was still there, but the feeling of loneliness faded, and her being was filled with a tremendous excitement and warmth. There was Adam, this new person in her life, someone who would be there always to talk to, to comfort her. It was a miracle. It must be love.

Lazily, luxuriating in the warm water, Carla took a bath and then puttered about in her room getting ready for Adam. Looking forward to the evening was a delicious part of the date, and she savored her anticipation, feeling feminine and catlike as she brushed her hair, changed the polish on her nails, examined her face in the mirror for nonexisting blemishes. She was almost purring, she thought, only occasionally being reminded of the heavy weight of unsolved problems she still carried.

Her father had gone out, she didn't know where, but now she heard Dan's familiar slam of the door, and his routine call, "Is anyone home?"

"I'm here. Upstairs in my room. Come on up."

Carla tied her robe securely around her.

"Where you going?" Dan asked, eying Carla's hair, already done up into a soft bun on top of her head.

"I'm going out with Adam," Carla said dreamily. "He's taking me out to dinner."

"You're kind of gone on him, aren't you?" Dan sat down in Carla's small wicker rocker.

Carla sighed, but she didn't answer directly. Instead she asked, "You do like Adam, don't you?" Her question was that of a mother who knows her child is beautiful.

"Adam's all right." Then Dan added unexpectedly, "But sometimes he seems so far away."

"I know what you mean. That's one of the things that I like about him. He always has something in reserve." Carla made herself come back to practical matters. "Dan, is Dad coming home for supper?"

"How should I know? I thought he told you."

"I didn't speak to him when he went out." Carla felt guilty. She had no business feeling so gay with this festering sore making a barrier between herself and her father. "There are plenty of meatballs left from last night. You can warm them up with a can of tomato sauce, and there's stuff for salad, and some of Hattie's pie for dessert. O.K.?"

"Sure, don't worry about us, we'll manage fine. Have a good time with your young man." Dan gave her a grin. "Drive carefully, be home early. . . ." His voice was mocking their father's.

"Oh, pooh." Carla gave him a gentle push out of the room. She was just finishing her make-up when Adam's car pulled up in front of the house. He was in the kitchen talking to Dan when she came downstairs. Adam never said anything about the way she looked, but his swift glance was an approving one.

They stayed talking to Dan, until Adam finally said they'd better go or they wouldn't get served dinner. Carla wondered if he felt the way she did, that it didn't matter whether they went out or whether they stayed in the kitchen with Dan all evening. Just having Adam there, being able to watch his face and to listen to his voice, their being together was all she needed.

But they went off in Adam's car. "We're going out to Hearthstone Inn, is that all right?"

"Oh, that's lovely." Adam had named a charming old inn set in a grove of tall trees outside of town. Carla had been there with her father and she had often thought it would be a perfect place to go to with some-one she cared about very much. She was not disap-pointed when she got there. The wood-paneled dining room was softly lit; intimate, but not overcrowded with tables; and at one end there was a huge stone fireplace with a fire blazing away in it. Adam had thoughtfully made a reservation, and they were taken to a table for two close enough to the fire to enjoy its warmth but not get overheated. Carla was smiling with pleasure.

"Happy?" Adam asked.

Carla nodded her head. "Yes, very." She was silent for a moment. "I should knock wood," she added with a laugh.

"Why is that?"

"I'm always afraid I'll have to pay for being happy afterward."

"And what if you do? Isn't it worth it?" Adam's eyes were holding hers.

"It depends," Carla said soberly. "I'd rather pay in advance, then I know what I'm in for."

"That would be deadly dull. Then you'd never take a chance on anything. I believe in not missing a thing. If you have to pay, those are the breaks of the game. I'm willing."

"You're surer of yourself than I am. That's the difference."

"I'm working at it. I want to be as sure of myself as your father is. He never lets his emotions get in his way, he's so cold and objective."

"He's not cold!" Carla was surprised. She had never heard her father described in this way. Everyone she knew spoke about him in great superlatives, and while Adam spoke with admiration, it was a kind of admiration Carla didn't take to.

"Of course he's cold," Adam said with conviction. "Look what he did to George Randall. It takes a very tough person to do that."

"But he thinks it's the right thing to do." Carla sprang to her father's defense automatically. "He wasn't being tough, he was acting on principle."

Sensing dangerous ground, they let the subject of Mr. Monroe drop, and Carla began asking about Adam's home in San Francisco. "It's the most beautiful city in America," he said. "You must visit there sometime. I'd love to show you the sights."

Carla listened eagerly to Adam talk about his parents and his younger sister and brother; he had never discussed his family so much before. "You would like them, I know you would. . . . Maybe someday you'll meet them."

Carla's eyes were glowing. She felt closer to Adam than she ever had before. When she let her hand rest on the table near his, he took it quickly in his own. "This is the most beautiful place," Carla murmured.

"And you're the most beautiful girl," Adam said unashamedly. "What I love about you is your enthusiasm. The girls I know back home are so blasé."

"I suppose they're much more sophisticated." Carla felt a twinge of jealousy. She would have loved to know something about the girls he had taken out, but she had more sense than to ask. She still felt that it was impossible for him to be seriously interested in her, a girl in high school, and yet when he looked at her the way he was doing now, she felt that he must be and marveled at her good fortune.

They sat a long time over their dinner. It was almost ten when, reluctantly, they got up to leave, and Carla decided the evening was the nicest she'd ever spent in her life. She looked around the room, trying to memorize every detail of it, knowing that she would want to come back to the memory of it time and time again. She would like to live in a room like this with Adam, the fire glowing against the soft wood paneling, the two of them having dinner together every night, sitting and talking. . . . They'd never run out of things to say, there was always so much to talk about.

"I wish we could go dancing, but then I guess it's too late now with school tomorrow," Adam interrupted her thoughts.

"This was nice, just the way it was."

In the car, on the way home, Carla sat close to Adam. "I wish this evening would never end," she said. "I was feeling so blue when you called, I felt awful. Seeing you made me forget all my troubles." She remembered the frightened despair that had hung over her in Ellen's kitchen early that day, and she clung to Adam's arm.

The whole evening seemed dreamlike, the warm

fire, the good food, feeling close to Adam, and now the dream was coming to a shattering end. Nothing had changed; her father had made a hideous error, and Ellen didn't want to be her friend anymore. Carla hurriedly poured everything out to Adam on the way home, telling him of her encounter with Ellen, and all the doubts she had about her father. She hadn't wanted to spoil the beautiful evening, but she felt compelled to talk to Adam.

"Can't you make him change his mind?" she ended up asking Adam. "My father thinks the world of you. If you told him you thought it was a mistake, he'd listen to you."

"You don't know your father. He'd think I was very impudent if I told him he was wrong. I told you this evening your father is tough. He's not sentimental. He's bending over in the opposite direction to treat George Randall like anyone else, not like a Negro, and not like his friend. He *wants* to be cold and objective about it, and he doesn't think Randall is qualified for the job. He'll stick to that no matter what. Until doomsday."

For a moment Carla wished she hadn't said anything. She didn't like to hear Adam speak that way about her father, and all her feelings of guilt came rushing back to her. It's just a circle, a crazy circle, she thought, trying to find comfort in snuggling up close to Adam and pushing away the panic that took hold of her when she thought about the growing abyss between herself and her father. She felt cut off, alone in the world, and she held on to Adam as the only real anchor that she could count on.

When he kissed her at the door Carla was certain that Adam must feel about her as she did about him. They clung to each other, neither of them wanting to be the one to say good night and to leave. When they finally parted, Carla felt so filled with love that she wanted to cry. As she went into the house, real tears were on her cheeks. Love was a happiness and a sadness, every meeting would be a joy and every parting would be another sorrow. . . .

She felt as if she had lived an eternity since that morning, and gratefully she sank into bed and went right to sleep.

CHAPTER 11

By Tuesday Carla knew that something was up. She had noticed Ellen and Eugene and a group of their friends in a huddle at lunch, and as Gadge said, "I don't think they're huddling over their algebra assignment, they all look too solemn."

It had been an uneasy two days for Carla. Ellen had been polite in saying good-morning and good-bye, but that had been the extent of her conversation with Carla, and her face had assumed the cool remoteness that Carla had first seen on it. Carla's emotions ran the gamut. When she first took her seat beside Ellen on Monday morning, she felt that she should make up with Ellen and that she would do anything to be friends. She had tried talking to her as if nothing had happened, but all she got from Ellen was a cool stare.

Then Carla started getting angry. This whole thing isn't my fault, she thought resentfully. Why should Ellen take it out on me? I went over to her house, I did my best, the next move has to come from her. If she doesn't want to be my friend, it's too bad about her.

If she weren't so supersensitive and stuck-up, she'd be better off. That's the trouble, the Negroes talk about segregation, but they segregate themselves. . . .

Her mind went on and on until lunchtime when she spilled some of her thoughts to Gadge. "I've done everything I could," Carla said. "After all, what my father does is not really my fault, and it's ridiculous for Ellen to give me the cold shoulder. What have I done to her?"

"I don't think you understand," Gadge said quietly. "I think Ellen feels she can't trust any white person anymore, and she doesn't want to be close to anyone outside of her own circle of friends. You've got to understand her point of view."

"But that's not fair. I want to treat her like anyone else, and I wouldn't take this nonsense from anyone. Why should I be so forgiving with Ellen? That's not treating her like an equal, it's treating her like a baby who has to be indulged."

"It has nothing to do with equals or not equals." Gadge's light eyes were intense and his narrow chin stuck out determinedly. "Ellen and you are different, and don't you forget it. She's had totally different experiences from yours, and they have taught her to expect the worst of white people! You're going to have to prove to her that she's wrong over and over again before she even begins to believe you."

144

"I don't know that you're right." Carla was impatient with Gadge. He was adding to her discomfort instead of making her feel better. "I'm not going to beg for friendship, not Ellen's or anyone else's. I think I've done everything I can, and that's it."

Gadge shrugged. "So that's it. Then forget about it."

But Carla couldn't forget about it. Ellen's friendship had meant a lot to her, and she had to admit finally that she had been flattered by it. She felt that she had cut through a barrier that might have stopped other girls, and it had been very gratifying that Ellen had liked her. But now she felt rebuffed, and she wanted to put the blame on Ellen as much as on herself, actually more. She told herself over again that she had done nothing to Ellen, so why should Ellen turn against her?

Carla could not accept Gadge's arguments. Surely Ellen had trusted her when they were friends. And I haven't changed, Carla thought. I'm the same girl with whom Ellen exchanged promises. How can she treat me this way? Carla began to wish she hadn't changed over to River High School. What good had it done, anyway? The whole idea seemed hopeless and stupid to her now. It would take millions of years for the races to trust each other and to become friends. How foolish she was to have spoiled her last year of high school with such a meaningless, feeble gesture as switching to this school!

Carla was very unhappy when she came out of school Tuesday afternoon with Gadge and Twinkey. They were greeted by a group of Negro students, led by Ellen and Eugene, handing out leaflets.

The leaflets announced a mass demonstration the following Monday with a march to the Mayor's office and to the office of the Director of the Mayor's Commission, Jake Monroe. The demonstrators would then throw picket lines around both places. The demands on the leaflet were for total desegregation of the school system, hiring of Negroes on the professional staff of the commission, and a guarantee that Negroes would be hired on the construction jobs of the city's redevelopment work.

"Boy, that's great!" Gadge said enthusiastically. He walked over and shook Eugene's hand. "We'll be there, don't worry. We'll get all of Lincoln High out too. Anybody handing leaflets out there?"

Eugene gave him a wide smile. "Yes, there are a few, but if you want to give them a hand I'll give you a pile to take over."

"Sure. Come on, Carla, Twinkey. You want to go over there with me?"

Carla's face was stricken. She kept reading the leaflet over and over again. "It says they're going to picket my father's office! I can't believe that they're going to do that. Eugene, why pick on my father? He's one of the best friends you people have in this town!"

"We have nothing against your father personally," Eugene said gently. "We just want some Negroes on that commission, and he seems to be doing the hiring. That's all."

"That's all! How do you think he's going to feel having a picket line around his office? How do you think I feel? I left a perfectly good school to come here, because I wanted to help. Because I didn't believe in any segregation, but when you do something like this I wonder if you really want to get along with the whites. You want integration, but you hate us at the same time, you don't care about *our* feelings."

Ellen was standing beside Eugene, her face pale and tense. She started to answer Carla, but Eugene interrupted. "If you're going to worry about people's feelings, think of Ellen's father, not being offered a job in his own town to help his own people. Your father can take it. The picket line is not going to do a thing to his income or to his life. It's not going to hurt him to be picketed."

"How do you know what's going to hurt him? If you could only have heard him talk about taking this job. Why, he gave up a good practice and a lot of money for it. He's getting a tiny salary, but he didn't care, because he believed he was helping the Negroes in town.

And now they're going to picket him! It's ungrateful and unfair!"

"It's pretty late to be talking about fairness." Ellen spoke in a cold, tensely quiet voice. "Why didn't your father hire a Negro, why don't you ask him that? Even if he didn't hire my father, he could have found some job for a Negro besides a file clerk! This whole argument is ridiculous. Come on, Eugene, let's go back to work." Ellen turned away.

Carla was furious and hurt. Bitter, angry tears were spilling over her cheeks. She faced Ellen before Ellen walked away. "I tried to be friends with you. I wanted to be friends, but you have a lot to learn about friendship. Friendship means loyalty, not jumping to conclusions. Why don't *you* go ask my father why he did what he did before you throw a picket line around his office? Maybe he has good reasons that you don't know about, maybe he *is* doing the best thing for your people. How do you know? You're so used to hating, to suspecting everyone, you don't know what it means to have a friend and to trust him."

The white girl and the Negro girl were facing each other, Carla's eyes filled with tears and Ellen's dark eyes bewildered, tragic, but controlled. "I don't hate anyone," she said, "and I'm sorry that your father may get his feelings hurt. But he made the choice and the decision, not us. I'm sorry, Carla, but that's the way it is."

Ellen walked away, and Eugene handed a pile of leaflets to Gadge. He looked at the white boy uncertainly. "You still want to go over there?"

"Yes, I want to go over there." Gadge took the leaflets from Eugene and walked up to Carla and Twinkey. Twinkey had her arm around Carla, trying to comfort her. "I'm only crying because I'm so mad," Carla said unconvincingly, wiping her face with Twinkey's handkerchief.

Twinkey and Gadge exchanged glances over Carla's bent head. "What are you going to do?" Gadge looked at Twinkey questioningly.

"I guess I'll go on home with Carla," Twinkey said.

Carla freed herself from Twinkey and stood up, erect. "Don't stay away on my account," she said addressing Twinkey. "I don't want to stop you from passing out leaflets, or demonstrating, or picketing, or anything. You do what you want."

"I don't want to do anything to hurt you." Twinkey's eyes were pleading, her round face creased with distress.

"Gadge doesn't seem to care about hurting me," Carla said, as if Gadge weren't there.

"I knew you'd say that!" Gadge's thin face was taut, and behind his glasses his eyes were looking at Carla with a mixture of pain and sympathy. "I'm not demonstrating against you, not even against your father. I wish you could understand this, Carla, but I've got to do it for Ellen and Eugene and the others. They need us more than you do. Eugene was right. This demonstration isn't going to make any real difference in your father's life. He can still have his job, his law practice, go anywhere he pleases, but it means a whole way of life for the colored people. I'd feel like the worst heel in the world if I walked out on this now, when they need every bit of support they can get."

"Do what you want to do," Carla said. She gave Gadge one long look, then turned away.

"Carla. . . ." Gadge made a gesture toward her, then shrugged his shoulders helplessly. "I'm sorry." He took the leaflets and slowly walked in the direction of the bus that would take him across town to Lincoln High.

"You don't have to come with me," Carla said to Twinkey. "Go with Gadge if you want to."

"No, I'll go home with you." Twinkey looked as if she were going to burst into tears any minute.

The two girls walked in silence. Occasionally they could hear calls of the group handing out the leaflets and the hubbub of the boys and girls coming out of school.

"I wish I knew what to say to make you feel better."

Twinkey looked sideways at Carla. "Maybe your father won't feel as bad as you think."

"I think he'll feel worse," Carla said gloomily. She turned to Twinkey with her fists clenched. "It's not only that. It's the whole idea of it. Why do they have to attack good people to get what they want? If they had meetings and lectures, they could educate people instead. I hate all this fighting."

"Well, I don't know. I don't really know very much about it, but I suppose if people haven't learned in all these years, Negroes have to do something to wake them up."

Carla didn't answer. She was so upset that she was saying things she hadn't really thought out. She was speaking out of anger and hurt rather than logically. Although she was grateful to Twinkey for coming with her, she suspected that Twinkey pitied her rather than agreed with her.

Carla felt desolate. She had always trusted Gadge's judgment, and Gadge had deserted her. She was deserted by everyone, by Ellen and Eugene and Gadge, everyone except Twinkey. The girls walked along silently, and when they came to Carla's house, Twinkey asked, "Do you want me to come in with you?"

Twinkey's sympathy was not comforting Carla. She needed to be alone, to cry her eyes out, to think, to try to figure out what she should do. "You're a darling, but

I think not. I have an awful headache, and I'm going to lie down and take a nap." Carla leaned over and kissed Twinkey on the cheek. "You're a good friend, Twinkey, thank you."

"If you want me to hang around, I will," Twinkey repeated, but her eyes were relieved when Carla shook her head and told her to go on. "If you want me, give me a ring, I'll be home," Twinkey told her. "And Carla, try to calm down. It's all going to work itself out, I know it will." Twinkey hugged her impulsively, and walked slowly down the street.

The house was empty when Carla went inside. She remembered that Dan had football practice and it was not one of Hattie's days to be there. Carla wandered around the living room aimlessly. She did have a terrible headache, but she didn't feel like napping.

She walked over to her mother's photograph on the mantelpiece. The picture had been taken when her mother was young, and the laughing eyes made her start crying all over again. If her mother were alive, none of this would have happened. Her mother would not have let her father do such a thing. She would have persuaded him to give Mr. Randall a job, and her father would be a hero, he'd be the most important man in town. Ellen and her family and friends would think he was the greatest. Carla let her mind wander away into a lovely daydream in which her father was acclaimed by everyone, and all her friends, Gadge, Ellen, Eugene, Twinkey, Hattie, and Ellen's family all looked up to him with admiration; they might even give him a medal or put up a statue of him, or name a new school after him. Carla would be so proud to be his daughter. . . .

She came out of her daydream with a start. She *was* proud to be Jake Monroe's daughter, she always had been. Surely now she wasn't ashamed? Then the idea came to her that perhaps she should make one last-ditch attempt to persuade her father to give Mr. Randall a job. Her mother could have done it, why not she? The thought pulled Carla out of her lassitude. She ran up to her room, got washed, put on fresh make-up, and dashed off to get a bus to take her downtown.

Miss O'Donnell, her father's secretary, greeted Carla warmly. "Your father's on the telephone now, but you can go right in. The phone's been ringing all day. Mr. Monroe's going to wear himself out with this commission. Everyone's telling him how to run it, but when you ask them to do something, they disappear. You'd better see that he gets plenty of rest when he gets home nights, he's working awfully hard."

Carla felt a twinge of guilt at Miss O'Donnell's words. Instead of taking care of her father, she had been another problem for him to worry about, but if she persuaded him to hire Mr. Randall, maybe then he would be left alone.

Adam was not in the office. Carla was disappointed, but relieved in a way, as she wanted to talk to her father without feeling fluttery. She watched his mobile face as he argued on the phone, his expression changing from impatience to anger, to good-natured laughter. "People really are funny," he said, putting the phone back in place. "All of a sudden the worst segregationists, the most reactionary devils in town, are worried about George Randall. When I ask why doesn't one of them give him a decent job with good pay, they get mad and hang up."

Carla squirmed uneasily in her seat. Her father gave her a shrewd look. "Don't tell me you've come to plead for George too?" Mr. Monroe had a frown between his eyes. "I was expecting it."

"Well, if everybody wants it so much why don't you do it? It seems so easy. I don't think it's anything to laugh about."

"Don't worry, I'm not laughing. But I'm sick of all these phonies suddenly coming to the aid of the Negroes. Where have they been all these years? I'm getting fighting mad, Carla, and don't you come here trying to heckle me some more. I'm in no mood for it. I'm doing the right thing, and George Randall knows it. By the way I made a date with that young Eugene

Ritchie for lunch. I want him to meet the architects and the engineers we're working with. He's a bright boy and they should know about him."

"If you think you're going to bribe Eugene and Ellen to your side, you're wrong. They're dead against you. They're organizing a demonstration, and they're going to throw a picket line around your office. I bet Eugene won't even have lunch with you!" Carla had never spoken to her father this way before in her life. She was shocked by her own hostile words, but she felt that she had to make her father understand where he stood and to face the fact that maybe *he* was wrong.

"Let them put on all the demonstrations they want. It's good. A picket line doesn't worry me. The more rumpus they make, the further I can go."

"Maybe it doesn't worry you, which I don't really believe, but it certainly worries me. How do you think I feel having all my friends, my new Negro friends, picketing my father? I've spent all my life thinking you were the greatest man in the whole world, and now I feel you haven't the strength of your own convictions. I feel as if—I don't know what—as if I want to run away and hide my face!" Carla's voice was trembling, and her face was tight with misery.

"Sometimes doing what people want you to do is an easy way out. Maybe you're the one who's failing me, did you ever think of that? I had expected some loyalty

155

and faith from you, but instead you're just like the rest of them, ready to assume the worst. Believe me, I'm glad your Negro friends are picketing me. I welcome it. If they scream loud enough, then the weak people I have to work with, the Board of Estimate, even the Mayor, will be strengthened. I'm not afraid of the Negro community. We all need their demonstrations, their impatience, it will wake us up and help us get something done!"

"I don't think you'll like it when it happens. I hate all this fighting. I don't see that anyone's getting anywhere."

Mr. Monroe looked at his daughter with troubled eyes. "You worry me, Carla. You and most of your generation. You want the world to be sweet and comfortable, and you want everyone to think alike and be good friends. You're afraid of controversy, you're afraid to be the lone voice in the wilderness."

Carla listened to her father with her eyes staring out the window. Now she met his steady gaze tremulously and tried to control her voice when she spoke. "How can you be so sure that what you do must be right? I never saw anyone so cocksure of himself in all my life! It doesn't even occur to you that maybe you could be wrong." Carla stood up. "There's no sense talking to you, I can see that. You are right and everyone else is wrong, and that's all there is to it!"

Carla's words frightened her so much that she ran out of the office and out to the stairway without saying good-bye to her father or to Miss O'Donnell. She ran down the long flight of steps and out into the street. She had never been so upset in all her life, and she had never talked to anyone like that before in her life, either.

Angry tears of frustration and helplessness smarted in her eyes. Carla felt as if the whole world were against her. First Ellen and Eugene, then Gadge—even Twinkey had only been sorry for her—and now her father. She walked blindly down the street, not caring in what direction she went. She wanted to walk and walk and walk, to walk clear out of town, to go far, far away.

She went past the office buildings, the small factories, and the groups of shabby neighborhood stores. Before she knew it she was walking on the highway, where there was no sidewalk, on her way out of town. What if she went on walking and didn't come back?

Carla felt in her pocket; she had two dollars and thirty-one cents in change. That wouldn't take her very far. She remembered reading a story once that said every child wants to run away from home sometime in his life. Carla had thought the statement silly when she read it. She had never wanted to run away, and as far as she knew neither had Dan. She loved her home, she had loved her mother, she loved her father too much, she thought grimly, putting him on a pedestal and thinking he could do no wrong. But now the idea occurred to her that it would be nice not to have to go home. She didn't want to face her father right away, and she really didn't want to be around for all the talk about the forthcoming demonstration. Everyone would think she was terrible not to join in, and yet she couldn't see herself walking in a picket line up and down in front of her own father's office.

Carla walked on, but more slowly now. The highway here was ugly, bordered on both sides by outlet stores, hamburger stands, a large sprawling furniture store with its windows crammed full of Grand Rapids furniture, and huge billboard signs. In sharp contrast the distant hills were beautiful, bathed as they were in the rosy glow of the sun just about to set. It would be dark in a very short while.

Suddenly Carla swung herself around. She had walked off some of her anger, and it was obvious where she wanted to go now. She walked very quickly, every once in a while breaking into a short run. She knew Adam was home in his apartment working on a paper for school, so she decided not to stop to call him. If she could only fly the long blocks over to his place. . . . She wanted to feel his arms around her, to lean against his shoulder, and have her upside-down world turn right again. She wanted to have the reassurance of his calm eyes and be told how much she meant to him.

She hadn't realized she had walked so far. The streetlights were on, and she was cold without the warmth of the sun on her bare head. Her legs were shivering in her knee-length socks, and she wished she had worn something heavier than a light windbreaker over her sweater and skirt.

She must look a mess she thought ruefully, with her hair all wind-blown and her make-up washed away from her tear-streaked face. But it wouldn't matter to Adam, he would love her just the same! That was one of the nicest things about being in love, she could relax and be herself and not worry about always looking her best.

Carla was exhausted when she finally rang Adam's bell. She had never been in his apartment before, and she was eager to see where he lived. It was a small brick house, and Adam lived on the second floor. When she opened the door to his buzzing, he called out from the stair landing to ask who was there.

"It's Carla. Can I come up?" Carla started walking up the stairs without waiting for an answer.

Adam's voice was distinctly surprised. "Why, Carla . . . for heaven's sake, what are you doing here?"

"I've come to see you," she said, facing him outside his door. "Aren't you glad? Aren't you going to ask me in?" She wanted him to fold his arms around her, to know everything she had been through that afternoon without her having to tell him bit by bit. In a book he would look at her face and that would be enough for him to open up his arms and comfort her.

But Adam was looking fidgety and embarrassed. "I wasn't expecting company, my place is kind of a mess . . . if you don't mind. . . ."

"I don't mind. I just want to sit down, I'm dead." She followed Adam into the apartment, and went directly to a low, comfortable armchair, sinking down into it.

The room didn't look very messy to her. It was a large room, almost square, with a row of casement windows facing the street. It was sparsely but comfortably furnished, with a studio bed, a large desk, now strewn with papers, a couple of armchairs, and lots of books. Next to the desk was Adam's typewriter, where he had obviously been working, and the only mess in the room was in fact the papers covering the desk.

"I'm sorry to interrupt you. You were working."

"Oh, that's all right. I can take a short break, won't hurt me. I've been at it for hours."

Now that she was here, Carla felt that something ghastly had happened. The visit wasn't at all the way she had pictured it, and she didn't know how to go about telling Adam that he was the only person in the whole world she could count on, whom she loved, and who loved her back.

They sat there looking at each other like two strangers, each one waiting for the other to open the conversation.

"What's the matter? You look upset." Adam was standing in front of the fireplace that didn't work. She knew all about it, because he had told her how he had tried it when he first moved in and had almost set the whole building on fire.

"Upset?" Carla felt as if she were going to laugh and cry at the same time. The thing was crazy. Upset! What an understatement! She was on the verge of hysterics, and Adam was calmly standing there, asking her if she was upset. The whole world had gone crazy, and she was alone in it.

"Yes, I am upset. . . ." And then she burst into tears. "Everything is awful. I don't want to go home, I don't want to see my father, I thought I'd come here and you would understand. I thought that you loved me, the way I love you. But you're acting so strange. . . ." She was sobbing too hard to say any more.

Adam's hand was on her shoulder. "I'm sorry, Carla. Try to tell me what it's all about."

Finally she was able to control her sobbing, and she told him about the planned demonstration, and how even Gadge had deserted her, then her going to see her

161

father, and the hopelessness there. "I walked way down the highway, and then I thought I would see you, that you were the one person I could come to. . . ." She tried not to break into tears again.

"I. . . ." Adam looked very unhappy. "I don't know what to say. I don't think you should have come here. I don't think your father would like it. . . ."

"I don't care what my father likes," Carla said recklessly. "But you don't want me here. Go ahead, say so."

"The truth is I don't." Adam's voice was very gentle. "I have a responsibility to your father, and, well, I think you're taking something more seriously than you should. After a good night's sleep you'll feel different about everything."

Carla couldn't believe her ears. "You're talking to me as if I were a baby, a little child. You're not the least bit in love with me, are you?" She looked straight into Adam's eyes, until he looked down at the floor.

"You take everything too seriously. The other night when we were out. . . . Well, you know, a fellow says the things he thinks a girl wants to hear. And I meant them when I said them, but you're awfully young, and I have a lot to do yet. . . . I can't be serious about any girl, not for years, until I pass my bar exams and start earning money. I thought you knew all that, and that you were just enjoying yourself the way I was."

"I guess I am a baby, and a fool too. No, I wasn't

162

just enjoying myself. I believed you when you acted as if you truly cared about me." Carla stood up. She felt dizzy and sick at her stomach, but she knew that she wanted to get out of Adam's apartment. She couldn't stand to look at him, to look at his things, all of the apartment so cleanly masculine, just as she had pictured it. . . .

"Now, Carla, don't start tearing yourself down, or me either." Adam's eyes were scrutinizing her face anxiously. "You make me feel like a heel, and I'm not a heel. I'm not the kind of a guy who goes around giving girls a big line. I've hardly taken a girl out this year. I like you, I like you very much, but I assumed that you knew as well as I did that we couldn't make any serious commitments to each other."

Carla was staring at Adam's typewriter, unwilling to look at him. "You want to get out of this scot-free, feeling very good about yourself. I'm sorry, but I can't go along with that. I don't know if you're a heel or not; I guess everyone has his own definition of the term. But I don't think anyone can assume that the other person knows he's telling lies. I suppose I am unsophisticated, but if you're so wise *you* should have recognized that. Good-bye, Adam."

Carla walked to the door. Adam put his hand on her arm. "Please don't go away angry. Go home, Carla, and think about it. You'll see that you're making a big thing out of something very slight. . . ."

Carla brushed his hand off and managed a smile. "Everything you say is making me feel worse. Maybe you'd better think it over. So long."

Out on the street it was cold and windy. Carla shivered as she walked for a block. The cold wind had become unbearable, so she went into a drugstore and called for a cab. She didn't care if she spent her last two dollars. She wanted to be home and in her own room, and she only hoped that she could get upstairs without encountering either her father or Dan.

CHAPTER 12

ELLEN walked around the kitchen nervously, waiting for the water to boil for her coffee. Her father and Aunt Hattie were at the large round table poring over a detailed map of the city. They were planning a meeting point for Monday's demonstration and the line of march the demonstrators would follow. Ellen was aware of the tense excitement in her father's voice, but she wasn't listening to his conversation. Her mind was on Eugene. Today he was having lunch with Mr. Monroe and some engineering and architect friends of his. Eugene had said he was cutting his study period right after lunch, but that he'd be back in school in time for his next class. He hadn't showed up yet.

Ellen looked at the kitchen clock anxiously. It was almost five o'clock. People didn't go out to lunch at one, and stay until five. Certainly not with businessmen, who had better things to do than spend time with a nobody little Negro boy.

The phone rang and she flew to it, but it was someone for her father, one of the committee heads with some questions about the demonstration.

Ellen's feelings about Eugene's meeting Mr. Monroe had been very mixed. "I don't trust him, calling you up this way before the demonstration," she had told Eugene. "It smells fishy to me."

"Don't be silly. What can he do? I'm no big shot in this demonstration, I'm just a high-school senior. I don't think the lunch has anything to do with the demonstration."

"Well, I don't know. You're president of the class, and maybe he thinks he can persuade you to call off the kids. I can't help but think Carla is behind this somewhere. If the high school weren't going out, she wouldn't be in the spot she's in."

"I think you're really going overboard," Eugene said good-naturedly. "Anyway, you can trust me. Nobody's going to talk me into anything. Forget it, Ellen."

Now Ellen was thinking of all the possible things that could have happened to Eugene. She hated the idea of his spending time with Mr. Monroe; in her mind she thought of Jake Monroe as the enemy. She felt that he was worse than the out-and-out segregationists, because he had pretended to be a friend, and now he had betrayed her father. She paid no attention to her father's reasonable arguments that he was not qualified for the job, and put them down to her father's own pathetic underestimation of his abilities. That's the trouble with us Negroes, she thought to herself, we always think the worst of ourselves.

"What's the matter with you?" Aunt Hattie looked up at Ellen from the papers on the table. "You're as nervous as a bride! What's eating you?"

"Nothing." Ellen stopped her fidgeting for a moment. "I'm waiting for Eugene to call or get here. He had lunch with Mr. Monroe today." There was no reason not to tell them.

Her father looked up in surprise. "What's he having lunch with Mr. Monroe for?"

Ellen shrugged her shoulders. "Mr. Monroe thinks Eugene's very smart. He was supposed to introduce him to some architects. But it's sure taking a long time."

"He wouldn't be having lunch all this time. He probably forgot to call you."

"Eugene wouldn't forget to call me!" Ellen said indignantly. "What a ridiculous idea!"

"You sure think you've got him hog-tied." Mr. Randall grinned at his daughter. "If I were a fellow I wouldn't forget to call you either."

Ellen smiled. But what if Eugene had forgotten to call? Maybe she should call him. No, she wouldn't give him the satisfaction.

"You can calm down. Here he comes now." Mr. Randall nodded toward the back door. Through the upper, glass half of the door Ellen could see Eugene take the porch steps three at a time.

"Hello, everybody." Eugene burst through the door, greeting the three of them, but his eyes were on Ellen. He looked very handsome in his dark suit, white shirt and striped tie, his face glowing with excitement.

"Where have you been? I thought you were coming back to school." Ellen looked at him inquiringly.

"I know, I'm sorry. I just left Mr. Monroe now. What a day! This is the best day of my life. It was terrific, I never had such a time!" He was breathless.

Ellen took a Coke out of the refrigerator and handed it to him. "Here, take this, and tell us all about it. You could have called me. I've been worrying about you."

"You know nothing happens to me. I couldn't call, I didn't have a minute. I met the greatest people. I'm telling you that Mr. Monroe is really a swell guy. He is wonderful!"

"I've been telling you that, Ellen. You wouldn't believe me." Mr. Randall looked at his daughter reproachfully. "I'm a pretty good judge of men."

"For heaven's sake, will you please tell us what happened!" Aunt Hattie looked sternly at Ellen and at Mr. Randall. "Will you two please give this boy a chance to tell us what he's all excited about?"

Eugene took a long drink of his Coke before he started talking. "They took me to a really good place

168

for lunch. I had fried shrimps that were out of this world—"

"Who are 'they'?" Ellen interrupted impatiently. "Who took you to lunch?"

"Mr. Monroe and two friends of his, Mr. Blakey and Mr. O'Day. They're from the engineering and architect firm that's working on plans for the city. The urban redevelopment program. Great guys, both of them. Well, at lunch they asked me a lot of questions, and we talked about a lot of things in building and stuff. I can't go into it all now, and you wouldn't know what it was about anyway. But after lunch Mr. Blakey asked me if I'd like to come up to see their place and see some of the stuff they're working on. Well, they drove me over to their office in Philly, and boy it was great! I spent the whole afternoon there, and Mr. Blakey drove me back here a little while ago in his Mercedes. Boy, what a car! We went back to Mr. Monroe's office. But what an afternoon! Their place is fabulous, and the stuff they're doing. . . ."

"Is that all?" Ellen looked disappointed. "So you spent an afternoon in someone's office. What's so great about that?"

Eugene grinned. "I haven't told you the best part yet. I saved that for last."

"Oh, you! What is it? You would tell us everything

except what's important!" Ellen pinched his cheek affectionately. "Come on, out with it!"

"Well, Mr. Blakey and Mr. Monroe started discussing my plans for the future. I told them I was going to the state normal school and that I planned to be an elementary-school teacher. They asked me if that was what I really wanted to do, and I told them no. Mr. Monroe asked me if I wanted to go to college, and I said I couldn't afford it. This way I could live at home and work and take some courses, but going away to a university and living there was out of the question. . . ."

"So what happened?" Ellen's eyes were wide with anticipation.

"Well, Mr. Monroe said, if he guaranteed my expenses, did I want to go away to college, and could I get in. I told him that the guidance counselor at school said I could get in most anyplace, and I'd probably get a scholarship. Well, anyway, Mr. Monroe and Mr. Blakey said that they personally guaranteed that the city of Thomasville would raise the money to send me to any university of my choice, and that all my expenses would be paid. They thought of everything possible, books, spending money, clothes, the works. They sat down and figured it out. They're going to get the Chamber of Commerce to raise the money. They both got so excited you'd have thought one of them was going! Isn't that the greatest! Then Blakey said that if

I do half as well as he expects me to, I'll have a job with him when I get out. He's already offered me a summer job if I want it. Ellen, me . . . little Eugene. I'm going to be working in an architect's office! I can't really believe it."

Mr. Randall stood up and put his arms around the boy. His eyes were bright with unshed tears. "This is a great day, Eugene, for all of us. I'm proud of you. And this is just the beginning. This kind of thing justifies everything . . . all the fighting and the pain. This is the important thing, what happens to your generation, Eugene."

"And what happens to our demonstration!" Ellen added dryly. She was looking at Eugene longingly, her heart filled with emotion. Yet she felt a chill of fear too. These white people would be taking Eugene away from her, he would be moving in a different world from hers, and she was scared. What if he found some white girl at a big university? Who was she to compete with the whole white world outside of their little community? They would have been safe together at Teachers' College.

"Oh, our demonstration will be O.K. Mr. Monroe thinks it's great. He's all for it. He says he welcomes it —the more the better as far as he's concerned. He's really a straight guy, baby, no fooling."

"I'm glad to hear you say that." Mr. Randall had a

proud look on his face. "I had faith in Jake Monroe, and I knew he was a friend. You can't make hasty judgments in these complicated days, Ellen. Look at Eugene now. His career is the one that counts. It's more important than anything Jake could do for me. I mean that, I'm not just saying it."

"Well, Mr. Monroe's going to get himself a fine picket line." Aunt Hattie chuckled. "He wants it big and strong, he'll get it big and strong. This may be a great day for Eugene—and it is—but George, you and I have work to do."

"I know." Before sitting down at the table again, Mr. Randall took Eugene's hand and shook it warmly. "I'm proud of you, Eugene. We'll all say we knew you when."

"You'll be saying it about your son-in-law, I hope." Eugene's eyes turned to Ellen. "You don't mind, do you, if I go away to a university?"

Aunt Hattie laughed. "I'll give her a good thrashing if she does. No girl can stand in the way of something like that." Her eyes softened as they rested on Ellen's tense face. "You'll see him vacations and summers. Don't look so miserable."

"I'm not miserable," Ellen said, but her eyes belied her words.

"You know what? I think I'm going around to visit Jake Monroe tomorrow. I want him to know there's no hard feelings between him and me. That's just what I'm going to do." Mr. Randall made the announcement happily. "I'm going to tell him that I know I'd be no good for his old job."

Aunt Hattie gave him a skeptical look. "Mmm . . . I suppose it's not such a dumb idea."

"Dumb? It's the smartest idea I've had in a long time."

Eugene was watching Ellen's face anxiously. "Come on outside for a walk," he suggested.

"All right." Ellen put on her coat, wrapped a scarf around her throat, and followed Eugene outdoors.

Eugene pulled Ellen's arm through his. The weather had turned foggy and warm; the fog gave the shabby street a theatrical air, as if the crooked buildings were part of a stage set seen through a layer of gauze curtains. The warm mist felt pleasant on Ellen's face as instinctively she and Eugene turned toward the river.

"You didn't say anything about my going away," Eugene said. "If you don't want me to go, I won't. I mean it."

Ellen shook her head without answering. They walked in silence for almost a block before she spoke. "I'm mixed up about it. Of course I want you to go. I know how much it means to you, and I think it's wonderful. But I don't like white people having to hand it to you. It's a great thing for them to be sending a little nigger boy off to college." She turned to him fiercely. "But it shouldn't be that way. It shouldn't be any *gift* anyone's giving you. There should be hundreds of boys like you going to the big universities, hundreds and hundreds, just like white boys. It shouldn't be any big deal!"

Eugene patted her hand on his arm. "Of course you're right. But, honey, that's the way it is now. And it's not going to change overnight. In the meantime, there are some people who *care*. That's the important thing. There's Mr. Monroe who cares whether I get to college or not. It's the beginning."

"Yes, I know." Ellen turned to him with a wry smile. "I'm also a little scared of your going off. You'll have all this fine education, and I'll be nobody right here at home. You'll be leaving me way behind."

Eugene stopped and turned around to face Ellen. "I don't want to hear such foolish talk." His voice was stern. "I love you, don't you understand? I want to go to a university, to be an architect, so I'll be someone you can be proud of, so I can give you the kind of life we both want, so we can be free people, not living in a segregated slum working at dull jobs, that we grow to hate. Don't you understand, Ellen? You are part of all this."

Ellen lowered her eyes before Eugene's pleading look, and leaned her head against his chest. He had his arms around her and held her tight. Finally she looked up and gave him a smile. "This fog makes everything so private," she whispered. "I believe you, darling. I won't worry about it."

"Promise me."

"Yes, I promise you."

They walked on. "I just can't believe it," Eugene kept repeating. "It's like a miracle."

"It's no miracle," Ellen insisted. "It's because you're you and you made such a hit with Mr. Monroe."

"I wish you didn't hate him so much," Eugene said. "It's really not fair. He's a friend, and we need friends."

"I don't hate him," Ellen spoke slowly. "I just. . . . Well, I just can't get excited every time a white person behaves decently. They have so much to make up for."

"That's true, but we can't be so bitter about our friends either. You got to get rid of that, baby, if we're all going to live together in this world."

"They're going to have to work hard to win me over," Ellen retorted. "Come on, let's not talk about race anymore. Let's talk about you and me."

Eugene held her hand tight in his. "I'm happy, honey, very happy. I didn't know I could be so happy. I feel that someday, when we're sitting by the fire in our own house, we're going to remember this day and this walk. We're going to know this was the day we could really plan on getting married. From now on, we both know it's for real."

"It's for real," Ellen whispered after him. The tension in her chest loosened and she felt a flood of warmth as she looked at Eugene's glowing face. His dream was coming true. She thought of their walk when it had all seemed impossible, and she was happy for him. She was his girl, and that was all that mattered.

CHAPTER 13

IT was Saturday, four days since last Tuesday, four days since Carla had walked out of Adam's apartment. Four days, ninety-six hours, five thousand seven hundred and sixty minutes. Carla had felt she would never be the same again, and now she was convinced of it.

The first day she had felt ashamed. Every time she thought of Adam, and the way she had burst into his apartment all disheveled, almost hysterical, she wanted to die. A dozen times she almost went to the telephone to call him and to apologize, but she restrained herself from doing that. The only dignified behavior would be to let the whole thing die. It was dead anyway, so why rake up the ashes? After a while the shame had turned to an empty despair and numbness. Without Adam to think about, what was there left? Being in love with Adam had given everything a point, a meaning, had given an intensity to every part of her life. The bright days were more golden, the rainy days cozier.

But with the despair also came the knowledge that she was being an awful fool. She had never had any patience with girls who mooned over lost loves, and here she was doing exactly the same thing. Her pride was nudging her to take it in her stride. She had been a silly, innocent kid, and she had learned a well-needed lesson.

Carla got up from her bed where she had been lying, and realized it was almost six o'clock. She had to go downstairs to get supper ready. Saturday night, and she had no date, no place to go. She felt rather luxuriously sorry for herself. No, not sorry, she decided, rather glad that she didn't really care. Here she was, a pretty girl, intelligent, attractive, and Saturday night, a whole line of Saturday nights stretching ahead, with no date, and she didn't care. That was really something.

The bell rang downstairs, and she wondered who could be coming in at this hour when it was almost suppertime. She heard her father greet someone, a man's voice, but not one that she recognized. Her relationship with her father had been a strained one all week. Neither one of them alluded to her visit to his office, which was fine with her, but she didn't like having this unsettled feeling between them.

Carla ran a comb through her hair, powdered her face, and went downstairs. The door to the living room was open, and her father beckoned her to come in.

"Carla, you know Mr. Randall, Ellen's father."

"Yes, we know each other," Mr. Randall said pleasantly, taking Carla's outstretched hand. Dan was sitting in the room, and Carla was uncertain whether her father wanted her to stay or not.

"I know this is a bad time to drop in," Mr. Randall said, "but I've been wanting to talk to you, Jake, and I thought I'd find you in now."

"I'm glad you came. Do you want to come in to my study where we can talk privately?"

Mr. Randall shook his head. "I have no secrets. Maybe your young people should hear what I have to say, I'd like them to." His eyes went from Dan to Carla.

Mr. Monroe made Mr. Randall comfortable in a big armchair by the fireplace, and fixed a highball for himself and his friend. Mr. Randall didn't waste time making conversation, but went directly to the heart of the matter, stating what was on his mind. He said that he wanted Jake to know exactly how he felt about the proposed demonstrations and the picketing of his office that was going to start on Monday, that they were picketing not against Jake but for the reasonable request that he add a Negro professional man to his staff. "I want you to know that I am still your friend," Mr. Randall said, "and I hope you are mine. I know a lot of people have been after you to give me a job, but I know, and you know, that I haven't ever worked in the field, and it wouldn't be right. I want you to be absolutely straight on this—I have never thought you were wrong about the job." He glanced over toward Carla and then at Dan. "I know some of the young people got pretty excited over it, but they don't know everything yet. There's a lot they still have to learn about what is right and what is wrong, and about the correct way to act."

"I went along with Dad on that," Dan said.

Carla didn't say anything. She had been so surprised to see Mr. Randall there when she came downstairs that she hadn't quite recovered from the shock. She loved watching his face as he talked; there was such a sweet warmth in it, so much humor in the twist of his mouth, even when he was most serious. As Mr. Randall spoke a warmth came into the room, a warmth that was pervading Carla, so that she almost didn't want to think about the content of what he was saying. It was enough that he was there, that the three Monroes could listen to his deep, low voice and watch his bright brown eyes move from one of them to the other.

"You did a wonderful thing for young Eugene, Jake, a wonderful thing. But that's not why I'm here. I'm not here to thank you, because I know you don't want to be thanked. I'm here to say that I know we're still on the same side, Jake. That's the important thing."

Mr. Monroe was very moved by Mr. Randall's words. Carla had never seen quite such a look in her father's eyes as he had when he grasped the colored man's hand.

"Yes, George, we're on the same side. And believe me, I hope those pickets are good and strong, and that they come in droves. I welcome them. Thank you for coming, George. This visit means a lot to me, a whole lot. We're on the same side, we always will be."

After Mr. Randall left, Dan wormed out of his father what he had done for Eugene. Dan looked at his father admiringly. "That's great, Dad, that's great."

Mr. Monroe looked over at Carla, but she was still unable to speak. There was so much to readjust in her mind, so much to digest, so much to think about. "I'd better get supper," was all she could manage to say.

Carla was silent all through dinner. Dan and her father talked about Mr. Randall's visit. "This is the most important thing that's happened since I took the job," Mr. Monroe remarked. "The best thing. It means a lot to me, and it's a lot more significant than all the things a twerp columnist has to say."

"It's great, Dad," Dan echoed. "Did you really mean what you said about pickets?"

"Of course I meant it. Don't you see? I need pressure and support. If I had gone out of town to bring a Negro on my staff, everyone would have been on my neck, the same people who are criticizing me for not hiring Mr. Randall. But if there is a movement from the right direction, from the people who really want my commission to be a success, then I'm in a good position to rally support and squelch the disrupters. A straight line is not always the shortest distance between two points. Sometimes, especially in politics and in this civil-rights battle, you have to take a roundabout way to get where you want."

"I think I see what you mean. Well, I'll bring out all the kids I can get on the picket line," Dan said. They both glanced at Carla.

She felt that they were waiting for her to say something. Her father probably wanted to hear her say that she had been all wrong and that he had been completely right, but she couldn't utter the words.

"You think about it," her father said, as if reading her mind. "Don't worry about who's right or wrong. It's more a question of how things work out and of being patient about them. I was gambling on being right, but if George Randall hadn't come here tonight I might have been dead wrong."

"I'm not really worrying about what's right or wrong," Carla murmured. "But I have a lot to think about."

When Carla opened her eyes Monday morning, she was glad to see it was a bright, sunny day. She jumped out of bed even before the alarm rang and turned it off. She looked out her window at the quiet street. It was so peaceful now that it was hard to imagine it filled with people marching, with banners, probably with voices singing, as it would be a couple of hours from now. Only the paper signs along the side of the curb saying *No Parking* indicated that anything unusual might be going to happen today.

Dan was up early too. She could hear him go into the bathroom to take his shower. Neither Dan nor her father had asked her any questions over the weekend, and she hadn't said anything, but she had made up her mind what she was going to do.

Carla took her shower as soon as Dan was finished, got dressed quickly, and went downstairs to fix breakfast.

"We're lucky to have such a wonderful day," Dan said enthusiastically.

"Yes," Carla agreed.

Dan gave her a quick look. "You going to school today?" he asked.

Carla felt herself flush. "No, I'm not." She was shy about telling what she planned to do.

Dan's face brightened. "You coming with me to the demonstration?"

Carla shook her head. "No, I'm not going with you."

Dan was bewildered. "You just going to stay home?"

Carla shook her head again. "Ask me no questions, and I'll tell you no lies."

Mr. Monroe was jovial when he arrived downstairs.

"It's a good day. They should get a big crowd out. It'll wake this town up. Come on, Carla, let's eat. I want to get downtown early this morning." For once her father was foregoing his usual breakfast ceremony.

"O.K., food's coming." Carla dished out the scrambled eggs and bacon evenly between her father and Dan, saving a smaller portion for herself.

Mr. Monroe ate quickly and left. Dan hung around uncertainly while Carla cleaned up and washed the dishes.

"I wish you would tell me what you're going to do," Dan pleaded. "I don't like going off not knowing."

"Wait a few minutes and I'll go out with you." Carla went upstairs to put on her make-up and fix her hair. She picked up her warm coat and ran downstairs to Dan.

"Come on, let's go." The two went outside together. The groups were meeting in front of the Baptist Church two blocks away. They could hear the noises of the demonstrators gathering already, and the streets were filling up with people headed in the direction of the church. They were mostly Negroes, but there was an ample sprinkling of white faces. It was a quiet group, walking in two's and three's, except for the young people from both high schools, who banded together in larger groups and were laughing and talking gaily.

"Boy, it looks as if there's going to be a real crowd,"

Dan said with delight. He hastened his steps. "Come on, Sis, let's go."

Carla stopped in the street and Dan stopped with her. "What's up?" he asked.

"I'm going to run over to Ellen's house." Carla spoke quickly. "I didn't realize so many people would be out already. I hope I can catch her. I'd like to walk with her, if she'll let me." She met Dan's eyes, and they smiled at each other.

"Go ahead," Dan said. "I'll wait for you at the church corner if I can. Then we can all walk together."

Carla's heart was beating rapidly as she ran off to Ellen's house. She's probably left already, she thought, and was tempted to turn back and follow Dan. Ellen would not welcome her at all. It was a silly, childish idea. But her legs kept going in the direction of Ellen's house.

When she arrived there, she saw Hattie and Mr. and Mrs. Randall coming out the back door. "Where's Ellen?" Carla asked hurriedly.

"She's inside waiting for Eugene. Go ahead in," Hattie said kindly. "She's upstairs fixing her hair."

Carla stepped inside the kitchen. The house seemed unusually quiet. "Ellen, Ellen," she called out softly.

"Who's there?" Ellen's voice sounded surprised.

"It's Carla."

"Oh." There was a brief silence. "I'll be down in a minute," Ellen said.

Carla walked around the kitchen nervously. She felt ashamed of the state she was in, acting like a scared rabbit, wanting to bolt out the door before Ellen came downstairs. Behind her she heard Ellen's voice.

"Hello, Carla," Ellen said quietly.

Carla swung around. The two girls looked at each other questioningly for a couple of seconds. Carla spoke first. "I don't know if you want to talk to me, Ellen, and there isn't time to go into a lot of explanations. I don't know that they would help anyway. But I thought. . . ." Carla could hardly get the words out. It sounded so silly now. She looked at Ellen helplessly.

"You thought what?" Ellen asked, her dark eyes on Carla's face.

"What I wanted to say is, if our fathers can be friends, it seems stupid for us not to be. I thought I'd like to walk with you in the march today. That is, if you don't mind. . . ."

Carla knew that for the rest of her life she would remember the smile that lit up Ellen's face. It was more than a smile. It was almost a new face, a face that Carla, even in her moments closest to Ellen, had never seen before. It was a smile of delight, of hope, and of confidence.

Ellen put out her hand, and in a second the two girls

were hugging each other. "If I don't mind!" Ellen laughed merrily. "Come on, let's go outside and wait for Eugene."

When the three young people approached the church, they found Gadge, Twinkey, Dan, and some of his friends, and they joined them. The Negro minister was on the church steps directing the crowd through a megaphone. Carla had never seen such a crowd before in Thomasville. It was different from any of the crowds that usually gather for parades or other city celebrations. It was a serious group, quiet, determined, and strong. They formed a double line and marched silently through the city to their destination. Gadge stepped beside Carla, with Eugene and Ellen right behind them.

Someone started singing the integration song softly, "We shall overcome," and soon the song rang out clearly.

Carla's throat filled. It was the most significant moment she had ever felt in her life. It was like being in church on Christmas Eve, when you felt close to God and to the people around you. She took Gadge's proffered hand, and turned around to smile at Ellen. She knew that she had come home to her friends, and she was happy.

HILA COLMAN was born and grew up in New York City, where she went to the Calhoun School. After graduation, she attended Radcliffe College. Before she started writing for herself, she wrote publicity material and ran a book club. About fourteen years ago she sold her first story to the *Saturday Evening Post,* and since then her stories and articles have appeared in many periodicals. Some have been dramatized for television. In recent years she has turned to writing books for teen-age girls. One of them, *The Girl from Puerto Rico,* was given a special citation by the Child Study Association of America.

Mrs. Colman and her husband live in Bridgewater, Connecticut. They have two sons, one of whom is married.

3718